Trespassers Will Be Shot

To Jim and Jane
Good Neighbors and
Excellent Friends

Ken Reynolds

TRESPASSERS
WILL BE
SHOT

and other short fiction

by

KEN REYNOLDS

Cephas Bradshaw Books

2021

ISBN 979-8-9852273-2-1
ISBN 979-8-9852273-0-7 paperback
ISBN 979-8-9852273-1-4 eBook

Cephas Bradshaw Books
Holly Springs, GA

For Marty

(Who has never been to Tupelo)

Appreciation

This book exists thanks to persistent encouragement from the members of my writers group. We shared many delightful, refreshment filled evenings where you gave me candid critiques to help improve my stories. I owe special thanks to Travis, Joyce, Bill, Vivian, Jack and Dave.

Although Fred, Harris and Tom are no longer with us, I will always be grateful for their contributions toward making the world better.

Thank you, Anita Rosen. Your keen eye for the trees continues to see the forest, and you get the credit for helping me bring these stories to print. Forgive me for ignoring parts of your advice. I bear full responsibility for any errors remaining.

Ken Reynolds
November 2021

CONTENTS

SOMETHING LIKE A WALK

After five dreary, wet days, morning brought sunshine and a sparkling bright spring sky—a perfect day for a walk. The day started just fine, but by mid-afternoon, I was worn out, utterly exhausted.

Age-related stiffness in my hands and legs made it a challenge to balance cereal and coffee as I shuffled onto the porch. But I did it. Watching the morning sunlight playing off the new green leaves creeping up the mountainside started me reminiscing about the times Marty and I rambled along the trails we retired here to enjoy.

We have spent a lot of time in recent months pacing about the house. An amble among the spring wildflowers held great promise for a leisurely way to shake off the dreariness that had settled into our home during the long grayness we both hoped was over, at least for a while. The thought of dawdling along looking for sprigs of color made my aging body resonate with memories of livelier years when our children enjoyed our springtime outings. They would dally here and there and then linger over whatever caught their fancy. They appeared to glide while chasing drifting dandelion seed their breath had caused to float away in the light breeze. I often found it necessary to step on my impatience to keep from interrupting as they wafted along, pursuing one more moment of delight. Watching our grandkids toddle about sweetens my memories of those earlier days.

I was savoring my second cup of coffee when hiking began to feel like a promising way to spend the day—you know what I mean, really hoof it, put a few more miles on the old boots. I don't wear boots much anymore, and something always causes me to postpone my next venture along the trail.

There is one problem with hiking—it makes me tired, and right now, my physical conditioning falls a little short of optimum. It occurred to me that instead of enjoyment, my hike would turn into lumbering along fatigued, like after one of those forced marches in my old Army days. Plodding weariness was not what I wanted to feel at the end of this beautiful spring day.

Moseying along the trail or meandering through a meadow and into the woods was more to my liking. That's always been a delightful way to flush away a case of the winter blues. Fresh air and exercise sounded like just the thing. I took my coffee cup into the kitchen and proudly told Marty about my exciting plan.

She said spending time in the woods sounded like a good thing for me to do, but not to forget my dentist appointment. Then, she suggested I use the park near the dentist's office.

Well, maybe so. Exercise is exercise, and fresh air is fresh air, but I didn't want to join those joggers and power walkers and their sweatbands and fitness strides. I wanted no part of a parade, not even watching one. The gait on my mind was more like a stroll, which probably would impede their roadside swagger. My vision involved perambulating across an open field or sauntering along a wooded trail, stepping to the beat of my own drum. Who wouldn't feel good traipsing through the countryside reveling in the sunshine for a few hours?

The dentist's magazines were old, so I amused myself by envisioning a ramble from times gone by. It is what I do while Marty shops. Settled in a chair or waiting in the car, I rove around from one fascinating spot to another, often getting lost in my reverie. The receptionist interrupted my roaming to verify what I already knew—the dentist was behind schedule.

To fill the time, I wandered out to New Mexico to one of our favorite trails, where my wife and I had enjoyed strolling along a riverside—our reward for traversing the switchback path down the canyon side. Relishing the euphoria that beautiful place evoked, I remembered the steep climb back to the top. There are some scary spots along that trail that require careful treading—a person can get away with an occasional wobble, but a misstep could be dangerous. I was considering the consequence of a tiredness-induced stumble when my turn for the dentist came. He has been my dentist for years, and I like him, but he's a talker, and today he yakked so much there was no way for me to journey back to New Mexico.

It was just as well because I was already tired. On the drive home, remembering all the rain that's fallen recently and getting wearier with each passing mile, the notion of trudging on wet ground and slogging through mud got less appealing. I parked the car, tottered into the house and shuffled to my recliner.

My enthusiasm for a walk in the woods had evaporated. All day long I had been busy locomoting from one place to another, and all that movement proved to be enough for one day. My walk in the woods will have to wait. Maybe tomorrow.

MUSTANG SALLY

Everyone knows humans can experience love for other humans and a few other remarkable creatures, but not for a machine. No one in their right mind loves a machine. Cars are machines—mechanical; therefore, they cannot love. Who can love something intrinsically lacking the capacity to reciprocate?

Not me. And so, I lived, seeing automobiles purely as transportation until one day, shimmering in the showroom lights, the Siren, whose name was Sally, lured me closer until I heard her whisper, "I've been waiting, just for you."

Everything but Sally disappeared. The wavering luminance of her glistening emerald body and vinyl houndstooth landau roof drew me closer, inviting my touch. I caressed her controls, and my heart raced with joy. I settled into the enveloping warmth of her soft interior, and she became my world, the one I did not know I was searching for—Sally, the Mustang I was meant to ride.

We became inseparable. The mountains, the seashore, from Florida to Canada. Together—that enticing beauty and me. Forty-seven thousand miles in only twenty months. I loved Sally. If anyone had asked me then, I would have said she loved me too.

I know! Cars can't love. But I learned they can be fickle.

One wonderful autumn afternoon, we wound our way along one of the beautiful back roads in the Shenandoah Valley. It had rained earlier, and through the scattered clouds, blue sky and sunshine made the wet autumn leaves sparkle.

It may be that while I admired the glistening autumn afternoon, my attention drifted from Sally's needs. Perhaps, she did it because I never called her name—what kind of guy talks to cars? Whatever the reason, after so many miles together, I felt her slipping away from me. She swished her rear end across the centerline, tempting an oncoming truck. I tried to steer her away, but all these years later, I can still hear her haughty, "Don't you tell me what to do" as she flipped her rear in the opposite direction.

Something—it may have been my scream—made her stop. But not until she eased her front wheels off the road surface onto the rain-softened shoulder. We both groaned as, in slow motion, she rolled over first onto her side—then onto her top.

Visions of movies with exploding cars filled my brain as I hung upside-down. Rushing to prevent catastrophe, I turned off the ignition. A horrible grinding noise reminded me that off is on when the world is upside down.

When I landed headfirst on her ceiling, I realized it would have been wise to open the window before releasing the seat belt. But some of us are constitutionally incapable of taking the straightforward way. Somehow, after wriggling around till I could get one arm from between my body and the roof, I put a hand on the window crank and lowered (or raised) the glass. I slithered, uninjured, onto the wet road.

I can vouch for how easily love can turn to hate. My urge to kick the ugly beast was irresistible. That heap of green junk, which the insurance company declared a total loss, had tried to kill me.

Our affair is long over, and my memories of that sassy contraption, and her swishy rear end, are not of fondness but personal dismay. How could I ever have regarded that car, any car, as other than mere transportation?

Looking back, though, I did learn a valuable lesson from my affair with Sally: Love is fragile, and like an automobile, a moment of carelessness can wreck it.

DETOUR TO TUPELO

Danny stowed his suitcase in the overhead rack and settled into the aisle seat behind the driver. That seat gave him the best view to assess the women waiting to board the bus. He had not seen one of interest until a tall brunette with a gray coat draped over her shoulders caught his eye.

She must have arrived at the terminal after the passengers began lining up because Danny had not seen her before he boarded. She was worth watching. Definitely.

She stood beside a small brown suitcase occupying her spot in the line, nudging it forward with her foot as the passengers ahead of her stepped toward the bus. Danny studied her thin, angular face. His traveling portrait photographer boss had taught him that her bone structure would make her look strikingly beautiful in photographs despite her nose being too large.

Her clothing was simple, a white blouse unbuttoned low enough to reveal cleavage. Her dark skirt stopped at her knees: nice calves and well-turned ankles. Danny liked small ankles. Although he didn't know the word, he admired the sheen on her shoulder-length dark hair.

She stood with her arms folded below her breasts, and Danny could not see a ring or any other jewelry. He listened as the driver collected tickets and confirmed destinations. The bus was a local, and most passengers were going to small towns along the way. The driver took her ticket and said, "Hattiesburg, Mississippi, change buses in Memphis."

The eavesdropper smiled. He knew the route, and he knew a lot could happen between St. Louis and Memphis. Danny had a talent. It wasn't a moneymaking talent, as his uncle Mike often reminded him. Still, in the mind of the almost twenty-two-year-old photographer's assistant, it was a wonderful gift, and he used it to make himself a very happy fellow.

She lifted her suitcase and started up the steps into the bus. As she turned, her coat slipped from one shoulder.

Danny sprang from his seat and gripped her bag. "Let me help you." She thanked him. He stepped back to make room and gestured for her to go ahead. She chose a window seat on the driver's side near the center of the bus. Danny asked if she needed anything from her suitcase. She said no, and he lifted the bag into the overhead rack. She wanted to keep her coat in case the bus was chilly. He told her he was sitting right up front and would be glad to help her if she needed it later.

She said, "Is Memphis home?"

"No, but I wish it was. I'm from Tupelo."

"I ain't never been there."

"Don't surprise me. Lotta folks from Mississippi don't know where it is, much less been there. But my friend Elvis is gonna make it famous. Where are you from? Memphis?"

"I'm from Hattiesburg. You teasing me? Do you know Elvis?"

"Yeah, but not real good. I mean, he's not my close friend."

She told Danny how exciting it was seeing Elvis on "The Ed Sullivan Show" and listening to him on the radio and how one time a friend of hers had gone to see him perform and all the women were screaming, including her. "I can't believe I'm talking to somebody who actually knows him in real life."

He said, "Hattiesburg. Well, I'll be. You know a fellow named Bobby Lee Pillow? He's from Hattiesburg. Me and him worked together about a year ago in Memphis. He was a card. Funny as hell." The woman moved her hand to her throat. Danny knew she had seen him looking at her breasts.

"No, I don't know him. I knew a girl by the name of Pillow, but her family moved away when we were little."

Danny heard the bus door closing and knew it was decision time for her. The driver's voice crackled over the PA system, and the bus would move any minute. Danny said, "You born in Hattiesburg? You don't sound like you're Mississippi."

She gestured as though pushing him away. "Oh Sugah, I was born there, but I lived in Chicago for a while. I guess the Yankee way of talking rubbed off on me. I been living in St. Louis for a while, but I'm glad I'm getting back home."

As the bus backed from the platform, Danny asked, "You moving, or just going home to visit?" She did not object as he eased himself into the seat next to her without asking if it was okay.

She paused, "If you're gonna sit here, I probably won't need my coat." She held it toward him. "I'm going back to stay."

He congratulated himself. *This one will be almost too easy.*

He put the coat with her suitcase and watched her turn her body toward him, crossing her leg and the skirt riding above her knee. She did not tug it down. He said, "That's a pretty coat. I like how it feels on my skin."

She said, "I'm glad you like it. I thought it was pretty when I saw it in the store, and it really keeps me warm. But I hope I don't need it in Hattiesburg."

They talked about how they disliked winter weather as the driver maneuvered the bus out of the depot and worked his way through traffic.

"Why did a girl from Hattiesburg decide to live in Chicago?"

She told him about a beach vacation at Gulfport, meeting a boy and falling in love, and running off and getting married. He got a job in Illinois, and they were happy for a while until he started fooling around. He left, and she was ashamed to go back home, so she moved to St. Louis. Now she was moving back home.

She did most of the talking. Danny asked questions, and she sounded glad to talk. His questions became more intimate, their voices grew softer, and their faces closer together. Less than thirty minutes into the ride, he kissed her. It wasn't much of a kiss, a little touching of lips, no movement, and no tongue. She didn't pull back, and he didn't move forward.

The driver announced the name of a town and a rest stop. Danny asked if she wanted to go inside. She said no, but she would like to stretch her legs. In the station, he bought coffee and a pack of Camels. Deep in the shadows of the building's canopy, Danny inhaled the sharp smoke, sipped his coffee, and thought about the pleasures of his job. He liked helping the photographer, but he was eager to get assignments of his own. He enjoyed visiting new places and meeting pretty women.

He watched the woman from Hattiesburg standing beside the bus smoking and talking with an older woman. When the driver announced reboarding, she dropped her cigarette and twisted her foot on it. Danny dropped the butt into the coffee dregs, tossed the container into a trashcan, and walked toward the bus.

She had reclined the seat as far as it would go and pulled the coat up to her chin. Danny grinned what his aunt June called his "little imp grin" and said, "You snuggling down for the night?"

She shook her head. "I got cold standing out there."

"It's November." He crossed his arms and rubbed them from elbow to shoulder. She offered to share her coat.

Her warmth spread over his arms and lap. They were quiet while the driver walked along the aisle, counted the passengers, and made his announcements.

Danny thanked her for helping him get warm. She said two people make it warmer. Danny agreed. He asked if she liked

Gulfport, and they were talking again. Each time she paused, he asked another question, a little more personal. They kissed. It was tentative and soft like the first one, but Danny put his hand behind her head and gently pulled her toward him.

Each break in their kisses brought a whispered compliment and another question from Danny. Her answers preceded more kisses. He moved the armrest into the space between the seats, and her coat hid their caresses. An experienced traveler would know what they were doing, but Danny didn't mind. He enjoyed knowing someone might look at this woman and envy him.

Danny moved his hand to the top of her stockings, and she squeezed her legs together. He eased his lips away from hers.

She whispered, "I don't even know your name."

"Danny. What's yours?"

"Selena."

He tried to move his hand, but she tightened her legs without taking her eyes from his. They talked. They talked some more. Danny learned she was two years older than him. Selena learned Danny was three years older than her.

He asked her to join him for the night in Tupelo. She said she had a ticket to Hattiesburg. He said they could change the ticket in Memphis and, if she was lucky, she might catch sight of Elvis in Tupelo, and there was a bus to Hattiesburg the next morning. He moved his hand and her legs parted.

The ticket change cost five dollars more than Danny had with him. He asked her to lend him the money until they got to Tupelo, and he could cash a check and pay her back. She hesitated, staring into his eyes. He carried both their suitcases as they rushed toward the last bus to Tupelo.

As the bus pulled into the Tupelo station, he explained that some friends were coming to meet him, and she would have to wait while they took him to get his car. She said nothing, but he saw a flash in her eyes and tightness at the corners of her mouth. They were silent for a long time, at least it seemed long to Danny as he waited to see his uncle's Ford enter the parking lot.

Everyone in the building heard her complain about having to wait in a bus station in a strange town where she didn't know anybody. Danny tried to quiet her, but she had no interest in why she couldn't go with him to get the car. He said, "Look! There's a nice restaurant called Woodrow's right up the street. Put your suitcase in a locker and go get some supper. Tell the cashier you are waiting for me. I'll meet you there and pay for it."

"Does Elvis eat there?"

Danny's usual high self-confidence faltered. Getting the car was a detail he had not thought through before asking Selena to join him. Borrowing the car, he would have to lie to his aunt and uncle. He had committed himself to more money than he had in the bank, and he intended to write a bad check. He felt like a mixed-up inexperienced kid. *Does one more lie matter?* He answered Selena's question, "I've seen him there a few times, but not since he got to be a star."

Through the open window, he leaned into the Ford and kissed his aunt's cheek. She said, "Welcome home, Sweetheart." He reached across his aunt to shake hands with Uncle Mike then got into the back seat. Less than ten minutes later, despite protesting he was not hungry, Danny chewed on the ham sandwich Aunt June insisted he have. They sat at the kitchen table while Danny hurried through what he had been doing on his new job. He asked about his grandparents and listened with genuine concern to the growing list of Grandpa's ailments.

Uncle Mike looked hurt when Danny asked to use the car to go to a party. Danny hung his head while his uncle told him he had no grace and no manners and said, who do you think you are showing up for a long weekend then taking off first thing. Danny had lived with his aunt and uncle since his parents died when he was eight. All three of them lived as though they were his parents. Danny explained about the party he was invited to and how it was past their bedtime anyway and they would have the next four days to visit with him. His aunt kissed his cheek and said, "Have a fun time, sweetheart. I'm going to turn in now."

When she closed her bedroom door, Uncle Mike said, "That hang-dog look ain't fooling me one bit, Danny. I saw that woman in the bus station. You mark my words boy, if you ain't careful you gonna screw yourself into bad trouble one of these days. Now you be back here and ready to help around here in the morning. Early morning." He handed the keys to Danny and turned toward the bedroom. He stopped and said, "You be careful, and be sure you use rubbers. You don't know what disease that woman is carrying."

Mike started into the hallway, but he paused and said, "And don't forget to put gas in the damn car."

At Woodrow's, the owner and Danny greeted each other like old friends. Sam and Uncle Mike were longtime friends, and Danny had worked in the restaurant while he was in eleventh grade. Sam nodded towards Selena, then winked at Danny. She sat at a table in the far corner. As he approached, Danny studied her scowl. He said, "I sure am glad you waited. I missed you real bad."

She handed him the dinner check and said, "It's time you showed up. While you're paying this, get me a pack of Pall Malls."

Danny swallowed. The bill was over six dollars, and he owed her five. The motel would be ten, and he had to buy rubbers and cigarettes and at least two bucks on gas. He took the check and walked toward the cashier.

Danny explained how he just got back to town and needed to cash a check, and he hoped Sam wouldn't mind holding it for a few days. Sam looked toward Selena, then back at Danny. "You sure she's worth it?"

They both laughed when Danny said, "They all are."

She insisted he drive by Elvis' house. When he agreed, she got over being angry and snuggled next to him and stroked the inside of his thigh. He enjoyed the fuss she made. "I can't believe I'm seeing Elvis' house. Do you think he's at home? Maybe, if you blow the horn, he'll come out so I can see him."

Danny stopped to buy gas. While the attendant pumped two dollars' worth of regular, he bought condoms from the dispenser in the men's room.

The glowing red neon "vacancy" on the motel sign startled him. The possibility of the motel being full had not crossed his mind. The isolated building sat on a little knoll about a hundred yards off the highway. For years, whenever he drove by the one-story building, it called to Danny. He liked that each of its doors was painted a different color, and sometimes he counted the cars parked in front and wondered what the rooms were like.

The clerk reminded Danny of a frog, extra-large around the middle and bulging eyes behind thick eyeglasses. Without looking up, he accepted Danny's money, grunted, and handed over a key and a receipt made out to Daniel Smith—the only last name Danny could think of other than his own.

Danny saw Selena's disapproving expression as she assessed the room, and he moved to take her in his arms.

She said, "I gotta use the powder room. You go find me a coke?"

From the vending machine in front of the office, he bought a Coke and a Dr. Pepper. He found her sitting cross-legged on the bed, filing her fingernails. She said, "What took you gone so long to get back with the car? I thought you ran off and left me."

He laughed and told her he wasn't going to leave her, but he had an argument with his friend, and he was sorry, but Lord, he sure did miss her and her sweet kisses, and he didn't want to wait any longer to feel that silky place he touched on the bus ride.

She said, "Are you gonna talk all night?

Danny was fifteen the first time he had sex. By eighteen, he was cocksure about which women were interested and which would be a waste of his time. But Selena surprised him. She didn't play games. She wanted it. She took him in her hands, guided him, and told him what she liked and wanted him to do next. She urged him to do this and do that, and she humped back at him and moaned and shouted. And she came. Lord God, she came.

Danny gulped water from the motel's little paper cups and wiped his sweat with a towel. He opened his Dr. Pepper and watched Selena propped against the headboard, smoking and taking small sips of her Coke as her cigarette smoke drifted across her face and up through the colorless shade of the small lamp above the bed. *Lord, she looks sexy and sophisticated, sitting there naked. And she really likes sex. Why can't all women be like her?*

He eased himself onto the bed beside and leaned against the headboard. Selena paid attention to her cigarette, and he didn't talk. He had nothing left to say. They had screwed, and soon, she would be on her way to Hattiesburg, and they would never see each other again. But he was thinking he would like to see her again because the screwing was great.

She touched him and said, "I think sweaty men are sexy."

They were doing it again. This time was much more than a repeat of the first. Danny was proud of his ability to keep going for a long time, but Selena was draining him with unusual ways to surprise and excite him. When it ended, all he wanted was rest.

Soaked in sweat, he sat on the bed with his back against the headboard, watching her as she walked toward the toilet. She closed the door, and he slid down until he lay flat on his back.

He closed his eyes and lay thinking about how tired he would be tomorrow. He felt her mouth, and his quick response pleased him. She straddled Danny and began rocking back and forth. He looked up at her face. *She really isn't pretty. She's downright homely. That nose is really big.* Her lipstick was gone, and even the dim motel lights did little to hide her smeared mascara. Through thinned makeup, he saw acne scars. *What am I doing here with her, and why the hell did I ever think she was worth risking a bad check? She's humping me to death cause she can't get nobody else to do her.*

She moaned yes and clasped his hair and said it again. She rocked some more and pulled his hair as she leaned back and yelled yes yes yes, then fell off him onto the bed. They lay quiet for a few minutes. Then, "You are something, Danny. I ain't never had nobody keep it going so much."

Danny was anxious to get out of the room and breathe fresh air. "I gotta go get us some cigarettes."

Selena did not speak. He repeated it.

"Besides, we used my last rubber. If we gonna do it again, I gotta go buy some more."

She screamed, "You sonofabitching lying no-good asshole." And more names Danny had never heard a woman say. The more she yelled, the more determined he was to get out. As he pulled his pants on, he stumbled and almost fell. He didn't bother with his socks and reached for the door, but she was in his face yelling, "You ain't gonna leave me stranded in this godforsaken dump."

The slap stunned Danny. He had a quick temper, but he had never hit a woman. He looked at her, standing there daring him to touch the door. He said, "I told you I'd be right back."

"You're lying pile of shit!"

He shoved her onto the bed and slammed the door as he left.

In the rearview mirror, he saw her naked silhouette in the light from the open door. She had one arm in the air, and Danny knew she was yelling, but he couldn't hear it and didn't care. *I gotta get away from her and get some fresh air. God, I'm thirsty.*

Danny bought a 7UP at the all-night gas station and talked with the attendant about the Ole Miss football team. In the men's room, he remembered Selena rocking on him and her breasts moving and how he felt inside her, and if they did it once more, he would break his record for one night. He bought another pack of rubbers, a Coke, and a pack of Pall Malls for her.

From the highway against the dark sky, Danny saw the lights through the curtainless window and open door. *That crazy woman is going to get us both in trouble.*

The curtains lay on the floor. The dresser was pulled away from the wall, its mirror broken. The chair lay on its side, and the sheets were half off the mattress. The bathroom was empty. Danny's heart raced, and his face burned. Her underwear and clothes lay on the floor. The gray coat, her purse and shoes were gone. But the suitcase sat where he had left it. He wanted to run, but he knew he had to stay. He lit a cigarette and thinking about his options.

I gave the clerk a false name, but he has to have the tag number, and the cops will find me if something has happened to her. Too many people saw us together, and as dumb as that clerk looks, I'll bet he knows everything that goes on here. Oh God, why did I get myself into this mess? Uncle Mike's right, I gotta stop thinking with my pecker. He finished the cigarette, ground the butt underfoot, and walked toward the office.

Two small lamps lit the gray walls and gave the black Formica counter a soft dim glow. A few scattered magazines, two maroon plastic-covered chairs were the only colors in the empty room. He assumed the clerk was in the toilet. He said, "Hello." Nobody answered. Danny waited.

He looked at the clock behind the desk. *Damn, it's almost four o'clock. I won't be worth anything to Uncle Mike. He'll figure I been out drinking all night.* Still, nobody came.

Danny reopened and closed the door, making noise and hoping it would get somebody's attention. He waited. Nothing. He said, "Anybody here?" Nothing. *I wonder if somebody robbed this place and kidnapped Selena. Nah, ain't enough money here to bother. I'll wait a few more minutes. Then I gotta let the police know.* He called again. Still no answer. He turned to go outside, and a soft noise stopped him. He listened. *Was that a moan?*

Danny walked around the counter toward the rear of the motel office. In a small hallway, he saw a door slightly ajar. A louder moan and labored breathing. *Jesus Christ, what if he's been shot? What the hell am I doing here?*

He peeked into the dark room. The breathing noise was louder. He eased the door open a few more inches. The dim light from the office lit part of a bed, and he saw someone moving. The size of the body told Danny it was the clerk. *My God, he's screwing somebody. I've got to get out of here before he shoots me.* As he backed away, Danny saw Selena's gray coat on the floor beside the bed.

He started the car, then remembered he still owed her for the ticket. He walked back to their room, put a five-dollar bill on the dresser, and covered it with the Pall Malls. He paused, then added two ones for taxi fare to the bus station

THE DOG

John. Wake up.

John, dammit! Wake up!
Uhhh

John, the dog needs to go out.
Uhhuh

John, get up and take the dog out.
Uhh, whatimesit?

John!
Ouch! You punched me!

I elbowed you. The dog needs to go out.
Christ, it's raining.

He's your dog.
He's okay.

You said that last night. Take him out.
Rain'll stop soon.

John. He's scratching the door.
O' alright.

I told you, if he pees in the house one more time, I'm gone and I mean it. Now get your ass out of bed and take care of your dog.

Crap!

SUCKER PUNCH

Ray Donovan holds his hand to his cheek, more startled than hurt. He has never heard of a sucker punch. All of the other surprises he has ever received were good things, usually from his mother or one of his grandmothers.

A moment ago, he had been talking to his neighbor. Now, standing in the empty hallway, the left side of his face stinging, Ray stares at the brass 3-B on Eli's apartment door.

He closes his eyes and replays what took place. He and Eli are classmates in Mrs. Collins' fourth grade. They walked into their apartment building and up the stairs together. They were talking—no, they were arguing about the best way to make a fist. Eli opened the door to his apartment, and something hit Ray in the face, and the door slammed.

He opens his eyes and rings the doorbell. Eli's mother says, "Hello, Ray." She doesn't smile or invite him in as she usually does.

"Can I talk to Eli?"

"Eli can't come out anymore today."

"Please, Miz Simmons. I need to talk to him for just a minute."

"Not today." She steps back to shut the door, and Ray sees Eli behind her—grinning.

When he enters his apartment, his mother calls from the kitchen, "Is that you, Ray?'

"Yes, mam."

"I have apple pie."

"Okay." In the bathroom mirror, the red spot on his cheek is smaller than he expects. He splashes it with cool water then holds a wet washcloth to his face. He wants it to go away so his mother won't see it.

He has one bite of pie left when she asks what happened. Ray believes his Sunday school lessons and wants to be honest, but when he answers, "I don't know," it sounds like a lie. His mother's mouth tightens.

"It's the truth, Momma. I don't know what happened. One minute I was talking to Eli, then bam! My face is stinging, and Eli's in his apartment."

"He hit you?"

"I think so, but I'm not sure. He must have. It happened so quickly. I tried to talk to him, but Miz Simmons said he couldn't come out. Ray searches his mother's face for signs of her reaction. She has taught him not to fight unless necessary, but she also taught him to stand up for himself and never allow anyone to bully him. He knew Eli hadn't bullied him, and there certainly hadn't been a fight.

At last, she touches his cheek with her fingertips and smiles, "You finish your pie and let me help you tend to that. Your uncle Jake is coming for supper, and we don't want him to see it. He might decide to break down the Simmons' door."

Ray likes his father's youngest brother, but he gets into lots of trouble—usually fights. The family laughs about Jake's craziness, but they worry because drinking triggers most of his craziness. Ray doesn't want his uncle to know what happened because learning that Ray did not defend himself will disappoint Jake.

Lying on his bed with an icepack to his cheek, he decides to say no more about the problem. Momma had told him to learn a lesson from it and be wary of Eli in the future. She did not say whether she would tell his father. It doesn't matter because Ray knows what his dad will say: "Leave it alone—it's the boy's business."

Ray tries again to reconstruct the incident. He and Eli usually walk home from school with other kids from the neighborhood, but today, Eli walked with some older boys. Ray lagged a few yards behind with two boys in his grade.

At their apartment building, Eli said, "Hey Ray, did you hear about the fight?"

"What fight?"

"Weldon and Joe, you know, in sixth grade."

"When?"

"Afternoon recess went around the corner away from Eagle Eye Ingalls. Weldon knocked him down. One swing. Bam! It's over!"

"Wow! How'd he do that? Joe's big. And mean."

At Eli's apartment door, Eli explained, "Weldon made like a roundhouse swing. See, don't curl your thumb. Keep it tight and straight. Makes a bigger surface to hit with, but it only works as a surprise cause it's like an extra powerful slap, not a punch."

Ray said, "I don't believe it works better than a balled-up fist."

"Does too. How bout what happened to Joe?"

They argued back and forth until Eli shrugged his shoulders and said, "I give up." He turned and opened the door.

Ray did not see the punch, but now he remembers everything. Eli hit him in the face and slammed the door between them so fast Ray had not seen it happen.

Eli had surprised him, but the blow had not even made him stagger. Uncle Jake knows how to fight; maybe I should talk to him about it. Finally, he decides not to risk Jake learning about what happened between him and Eli. He knows his uncle's only concern will be how Ray intends to get revenge.

Ray has been in one fight, although they had not actually fought. At the beginning of second grade, an older and much bigger boy shoved and tormented Ray for several days. His seething anger exploded when the bully punched him in the face. He had used a stick, and the first blow hit his persecutor on the shoulder, and the second scraped the boy's back as he turned and ran. The bullying stopped, and Ray liked that.

Ray's family had moved into the Clancy Street apartment when his father returned from overseas after the war. Eli and his mother lived across the hall, and the boys became friendly but not close. Eli has no interest in baseball, but Ray loves the game, and Eli prefers reading the Wizard of Oz, while Ray reads about Babe Ruth and Lou Gehrig. The boys are in the same fourth-grade class, but Eli studies or goes to the library after school while Ray finds something physical to occupy his time. Ray has never thought of Eli as a fighter, and until today, never heard him mention fighting.

Embarrassed and angry, Ray doesn't understand why Eli hit him, but he knows he cannot let Eli get away with it. His anger deepens each time he rethinks the incident. *What if Eli tells somebody at school?* Ray's stomach flutters. *Thank God, tomorrow is Saturday.* Before the bathroom mirror, he examines his face and announces to his reflection, "I'm gonna get that S.O.B. I'll teach him not to mess with me."

The red spot fades away before Ray's father gets home, and his mother does not mention the incident. Jake arrives for supper, and their light, cheerful conversation is mostly about family in Texas, some of their old neighbors, and the weather. His father and uncle decide tomorrow will be a good day to go fishing, and to Ray's delight, they include him in the plans.

Saturday morning, during the drive to the lake, Ray broods on Eli and convinces himself a simple fight will not be revenge. While they fish, he breaks his resolution and tells his dad and uncle about Weldon and Joe but does not mention the incident with Eli. His father says the flat fist sounds like a glorified slap. Jake says, "It might be okay for a sucker punch, but not in a real fight."

On the way home, agonizing about being a "sucker," Ray works on a plan. *I'll show him a real sucker punch, no crazy open fist stuff.* The more he broods, the more determined he is to hurt his attacker. *The bastard deserves no mercy and punching him in the nose when he answers the door is too tame. Anyway, Miz Simmons always answers the door.*

Early Sunday morning, a nightmare startles Ray awake. He sits on the edge of the bed, his heart racing and his face cold and sweaty. He tries to shake off his dream of ambushing Eli. As his nemesis goes by, Ray calls his name and swings his baseball bat. Eli turns, then drops to the sidewalk—dead.

In the bathroom, Ray washes his face and stares at his reflection in the mirror. *You can't risk killing him, so you have to come up with something else.* Back in bed, his skin is clammy with sweat, and he can't get comfortable.

At eight o'clock, his mother reminds him to get ready for their monthly Sunday visit to his grandparents. Ray is glad they will not be going to church because he feels guilty about the dream and knows Sunday school will make him feel worse, and he wants revenge, not forgiveness. He looks forward to playing with his cousins, and he loves Grandma Donovan's cooking. There will be plenty to keep his mind off Eli and the terrible nightmare. They get home after dark, and he has not seen Eli all weekend.

On Monday, the enemy does not come to school. At recess, Ray talks with a fifth grader with a reputation for fighting. He hopes to learn more about surprising people with a sucker punch, but the boy offers nothing Ray has not already considered. After school, he goes straight home and stays inside to avoid Eli.

Eli is not in school on Tuesday, and that afternoon, Ray plays catch with a friend, and neither boy mentions their neighbor.

On Wednesday, he asks some classmates about Eli, but no one has seen him. At supper, he asks, "Momma, is Eli sick? He hasn't been in school." His parents look at each other, and Ray almost misses his father's slight nod. His mother says, "They moved away on Saturday, and Mrs. Simmons did not want anyone to know they were leaving."

"Why?

"The Simmons have a problem ... "

"What kind of problem? I don't understand." He looks from one stone-faced parent to the other.

His father says, "You know Eli's father died."

"Yes, sir, but that was in the war, and it's been a long time."

"Barely a year, son. That seems like a long time at your age." His parents look at each other until Ray almost gives up getting an answer to his question.

At last, his father continues, "Eli and his mother have no other family. Mrs. Simmons took a job when Mr. Simmons went into the army, but when the soldiers came home, she had to give it up."

"But why? What did her job have to do with the war ending?"

"The people who worked at the factory before the war were all men. Because so many were away fighting, the company hired women to replace them. As the men returned from overseas, the company rehired them, and the women were let go."

"Let go where?"

"That's a nice way of saying fired," his mother says.

"The upshot, Ray, is because Mr. Simmons died fighting in the war, management kept Eli's mother as long as they could. But they finally had to let her go, and she couldn't find another job. She no longer had enough money to pay the rent, and they had to move," his father says.

"But where did they go?"

"No one knows."

THE LAST LINK

The odor repelled Ray. Memories of his mother dying in this nursing home still weighed on him, but he was eager to see Jake. His father's youngest brother had always been the primary source of laughter and tears for the Donovan family. Now he was Ray's last living older relative. At Jake's door, he peered in. "Hey Jake, how's it going?"

"Well, looky here, my favorite nephew, Raymond Donovan. Come on over here." The old man lying on the bed grinned at a petite, gray-haired nurse removing a blood pressure cuff from his arm. "Hang on to your panties, Glenda. This is the boy I've been telling you about. He'll be after you straight out."

"He can't be worse than you are, Mr. Donovan."

"Don't you believe it. I taught him the ropes, but he's a lot smarter than me. He's got two college diplomas and probably has more experience too. But he's not as good-looking as me, is he?"

The nurse smiled and extended her hand. "Mr. Donovan, I'm Glenda Tillman. Everyone here feels they already know you. Your uncle talks about you all the time. Welcome."

"I'm pleased to meet you. I'm sure you know not to believe a word the old coot says. I hope he isn't too much of a bother; don't kick him out. No one else wants him, and I'll be stuck with the job."

The nurse laughed and excused herself as Ray clasped his uncle's extended hand with both of his. "Sounds like you're up to your old tricks, Jake."

"Don't intend to stop. No reason to, and lots of reasons not to. It's good to see you, Ray."

Jake looked much older than Ray expected. The old man's broad smile made his mouth appear exceptionally large on his frail face. His long-ago capped teeth were unnaturally white against the yellow-tinged skin drawn tight across his cheekbones. His smile was as winning as ever, but the full, once sensual, lips had become thin colorless lines. Ray remembered slightly protruding brown eyes sparkling with the fire of life, but now they were hazy and sunk deep under bushy white eyebrows.

He moved a chair closer to his uncle's bed and glimpsed the scar on Jake's scalp. The thin white hair no longer concealed what Grandma Donovan maintained caused Jake's erratic behavior. The family knew his behavior caused the scar, but no one dared challenge Grandma.

Jake Donovan had been legendary in honky-tonks and pool halls from Orlando to Houston, a man whose father described as loyal as the Dobermans he raised and volatile as the rattlesnakes he hunted. Jake seemed to attract troubles, but they always bothered other people more than they did Jake.

Ray's mother and wife said Ray was naïve, and his friendship with his father's youngest brother confounded them. Both women saw Jake as nothing more than an unreliable drunk who enjoyed getting into fights.

Ray did not pretend to understand. He knew Jake drank too much and too often. Yes, he made promises he could not keep and some he never intended to keep. Ray disagreed about the other charge. Jake was abrasive, but he did not start fights. They erupted when he was challenged or when he saw someone abusing a weaker person. Ray admired that about his uncle, especially his willingness to endanger himself for other people.

"It's been a long time, Ray. How you doing? You have a fancy time over there with the Queen and all of them English folks?"

"England's fine, Jake. They have great beer, but I'm glad to be home. Tell me what's going on. What are you doing in this place? Are they treating you okay?"

The old man's smile faded, "Yeah. They treat me fine, ... but ... my eyes keep getting worse. It's got to where I can't do the stuff I need to do at home. Mostly I can't clean the house or myself. Then my stomach, you know, that diverticular stuff I've had for years put me in the hospital, and I had a stroke. I guess I'm falling apart. Dr. Jackson said I was lucky to be in the hospital when it happened. I was there for two weeks, then he sent me to this joint here, and I've been here forever. I'm ready to go home—but I guess it ain't gonna happen. And they won't even give me any bourbon." The old man closed his eyes, and his smile faded into a straight line.

An unexpected sadness swept through Ray. There had been a dramatic change since he last saw his uncle. The man had always loved talking face to face, but he never wrote letters or initiated telephone calls. The few times Ray had called him, Jake was upbeat, and he never complained. Between the London assignment and brooding about his broken marriage, he had not thought about Jake's health. He knew Jake could tolerate adversity as long as he could have fun. But when the fun stopped, Jake found a way to make the situation different—whether better or worse was unimportant. Ray wondered how long Jake would tolerate being bedridden in a nursing home.

He remembered Doctor Jackson's telephone call to London, "Your uncle had a stroke. He's not in immediate danger, but his left side is weak, and he can't walk. He's old and depressed, Ray. He wants to see you, and I think it will help."

Jake whispered, "Ray, I'm sorry about Peg and the baby. I know it's tearing you apart inside."

"It's not easy, but you know that. You're divorced."

Jake grinned. "Several times."

You make it seem so casual Jake. I've tried, but I can't do it."

"Oh, hell I know that, but with me, it's different. I'm a rambler, and I've been married more times than I can remember. I even forgot how many times me and Toots got hitched."

"You married her three times that I know of."

"Yeah, at least three. Unbelievable woman—make a man do anything. I still love her, and she's been dead a long time."

Ray knew Jake was telling the truth. As soon as Ray learned to walk, he and his uncle fished every lake and stream within a hundred miles of Montgomery—often accompanied by Ray's father and grandfather. On those fishing trips, Jake talked freely about his work and the people who hired him to paint and wallpaper their houses, but in his tales, Jake always got a laugh by referring to himself as a decorator. He talked about the barroom brawls, his troubles with women, and how much Toots meant to him.

Tears glistened in the old man's eyes, and he wiped them with the sleeve of his faded blue pajamas. "I got kids I don't even know and don't want to know. It's different with you. You're serious."

"I suspect I'm more like you than you know."

"Ain't nobody like me, Ray. For the first time in my life, I'm acting like you—serious. What were you 'bout thirty-two when you married Peg?"

"Thirty-one, but that's close enough."

"See what I mean, serious and precise. Waited for the right woman, and you expected it to last—I never expected any of mine to last." His voice grew softer. A melancholy sadness replaced the enthusiasm of a few minutes before. Jake sighed, closed his eyes, and drifted into sleep. His chest moved with the soft regular rhythm of a sleeping child.

The imagery made Ray smile. Childlike was how he thought of Jake. A good, intelligent man whose sense of right and wrong never fully developed. The world was rosy until he got angry, and throughout his life, the anger came with alarming unpredictability.

He never set out to hurt anyone and would not carry a weapon, but he plunged in with his fists when wronged or provoked.

Ray studied the faded scars around his uncle's eyes and on his cheekbones. His zigzag nose had become more prominent with age, and a jagged line still showed, where fifty years ago, a broken beer bottle raked across his left cheek. Jake's hands rested on his stomach. Ray marveled at the enlarged knuckles and twisted fingers from decades of arduous work, arthritis, and fighting.

In 1941, Jake convinced his parents to allow him to enlist in the Army. Grandpa Donovan joked that only Grandma needed convincing because he was ready to turn Jake over to someone else by the time the boy was three years old. When Jake and the Army had a disagreement, his parents were not surprised. Ray's eyes moved to the old man's scalp. Less than six months after enlistment, Jake was court-martialed and sentenced for an offense Ray never heard specified—except by Jake himself.

In Jake's version, he got caught making out with a colonel's daughter, and the Army charged him with attempted rape. He commandeered a jeep and made a daring escape attempt, but the MPs fired at him as he drove through the base gate. He was never specific whether their bullets hit him or the jeep, but his skull required extensive repair when they pulled Jake from the wreckage. He spent a long time in the hospital, served his sentence, and was dishonorably discharged.

He liked to say he earned the silver metal in his skull for demonstrating the stupidity of the United States Army. Grandma Donovan often said, "My son was injured while serving his country and has a silver plate in his skull." Until her death, she insisted the plate caused pressure on Jake's brain and made him do crazy things. His brothers insisted the craziness came first and was the reason he wound up with the plate. But they conceded that a bullet may still be in his head, causing lead poisoning.

Jake opened his eyes. "What's so damned funny. Have you been stuck in a nursing home lately? No bourbon. No beer. No cigarettes. I'm telling you, it ain't funny."

"I just remembered the day you bounded into Grandma's kitchen to get everybody to admire your shiny new '47 Ford. You marched the family into the backyard. After everybody oohed and aahed, you whacked the fender with Grandpa's sledgehammer."

"I still think it's dumb to drive around worrying about getting the first dent in a new car. Better just to get it over with."

"I never asked, but have you done that to all your new cars?"

"Cheaper to buy what the rich folks get rid of after a year or two. Anyway, I never could afford another new one."

"I never understood how you afforded that one."

"Me neither, but back then, I bought whatever I wanted. It didn't work so well in the long run, but it don't matter now. Life has been fun."

When the laughing stopped, Jake said, "Are you gonna talk to me about Peg?"

"I'm not sure what to say, Jake. She couldn't put up with my being gone so much. And she would not move to London."

"When you two married, she knew the government might send you anywhere."

"Yeah, but she changed after we'd been married a while. She suspected all kinds of stuff—not without reason. I made a mistake; she found out and couldn't let go of it. She got pregnant about the time the London job came up. She convinced herself that I took the job just to chase women and refused to believe that turning it down would have meant the end of my career. We had a big fight, and she went home to her parents in Chicago." Ray had not wanted to burden his uncle with the details of the agonizing battle raging in his mind.

"And the baby?"

"That's the hard part. I got over Peg sooner than I expected, but not the baby. How can you miss a baby you've never known?"

"Hell, Ray, you're asking the wrong man. I never had that problem. I already taught you everything I know, and I got no answers for you. I guess you have to just get on with your life. It's too damned short to waste. Momma might be right about this plate in my head. I never miss nobody except her and Toots. I miss you, but that's different. You take me the way I am and don't try to get me to be somebody else."

"I know better."

"I specially don't miss kids I never saw. But what the hell. I'm the black sheep, and you're the responsible one. You know Momma loved you more than all her other grandkids put together. You're conscientious and dependable enough to make up for me and at least two or more people."

"Yeah, I try to be conscientious, Jake, but I know you were Momma's baby. From what I heard and what I saw, she spoiled you rotten. If something went wrong, no matter what you did, she never blamed you. I also know you loved her enough to make up for everything you did—well, almost." Ray winked at his uncle, and a broad smile lit the old man's face.

A knock on the door interrupted them, and Dr. Jackson strode in. Ray shook hands and excused himself, knowing Jake would want privacy with the doctor. He found the men's room and some coffee and settled into a chair. He was taking his first sip when the doctor approached. Stanford Jackson was seventy-three and ready to retire, but he had been the Donovan family physician since before Ray was born.

He smiled, "I'm glad you're here, Ray. Jake has perked up since you called to say you were on your way."

"I'm sorry I couldn't get here sooner. What can you tell me?"

"Jake wants me to tell you everything." The doctor motioned for Ray to sit while he poured coffee for himself. "He has good times and tough times. He'll be alert for a while, but he tires quickly and loses ground. He needs a reason to keep going, but it's going to take more than desire. He is not improving, and his body is giving out."

Ray smiled, "You mean finally giving out?"

"Perhaps you're right. The man is remarkable. Most people couldn't have survived all he has done to himself or what's been done to him. Amazingly, he has accomplished both."

"Is there anything I can do?"

"Spend time with him and try to keep his spirits up. There are a lot of things wrong. His digestive system has been a problem for nearly forty years. He'd been drinking the night we admitted him to the hospital. You can't do that when you have cirrhosis. Did you notice jaundice?"

Ray nodded, "Yes, but I've seen him yellow-tinged so many times I ignored it. I guess I've been concentrating on the stroke."

"The stroke was a warning. He's a prime candidate for another. He tells me he has quit smoking, but I know better. His cholesterol is too high, and his blood pressure is responding poorly to medications." The doctor paused, "He is alert today, but he hasn't improved since we moved him from the hospital. Ray, you're his closest relative, and you need to know he's in a precarious situation. He may last a long time, but he could go anytime."

The doctor sipped coffee while Ray absorbed the news. Ray had often thought about Jake's drinking and eating habits, but he was not prepared for this additional information. Jake was supposed to be indestructible.

"Is there anything you can do? Should he be in the hospital?"

"At this point, we can do everything he needs here, and the hospital is next door. His age, general health, and living habits make a liver transplant out of the question. His kidney function is declining and—well, you know what that means." He paused, put his hand on Ray's shoulder, "I'm sorry, Ray. I've known your family a long time—you folks have been my patients since I started practicing. I know how fond you are of Jake. I don't have to tell you it's a wonder he's still with us. My partners and I will do everything we can do to help him—we'll make it as easy for him as we can."

"I know you will. Is he in pain? He doesn't act like it."

"He is, but the man has a remarkable tolerance for discomfort, and he rarely asks for pain relief." He chuckled and shook his head, "Yesterday, he asked for bourbon—again. I'm not kidding, and neither was he."

"My uncle always is a man on a mission about bourbon."

While Jake slept, Ray leaned against the sun-warmed recliner cushions and felt the tension in his flight-weary back ease. Fleeting memories of fishing and laughter and food danced in his mind. The times at his grandparent's house with the four brothers and twelve cousins represented Ray's ideal of happiness, he tried to bring them into focus, but they remained formless impressions— the crowded house, Grandpa's smile, and Grandma working in the kitchen. Ray ached for those happy times. Jake's brothers were dead, and he regretted not keeping up with his cousins. He didn't know how to contact his uncle's ex-wives or children.

Am I going to let my son slip away too? Ray's eyes brimmed. Recurring tears had embarrassed him at work. They came when he thought about the baby or when a co-worker talked about her lost dog or his boss urged him to get help. The sadness was overtaking him again.

Why do I always put myself first—even before Peg and my son. He turned toward the window and watched the longest day of his life day fade into darkness.

You're right, Jake, I am serious, but I'm also a lot like you. Don't go yet. You're my last link to happiness.

FACING THE STORM

Ray sits on the stern seat of his candy-apple-red outboard, elbows resting on his knees, watching water flow out the drain. He reinserts the plug, screws it down tight, and taps Eddie on the shoulder, "Okay, it's beer o'clock."

Eddie eases the throttle back, shifts to neutral, and shuts off the engine. The big outboard makes the stern sit low in the water, but the fiberglass boat rocks gently with the motion of the waves.

Ray hands a beer to each of his friends and says, "These are the last ones." He leans on the transom seat, pulls the pop-top on his beer, and waits for the inevitable argument to begin.

Eddie says, "The last beers. Dammit, Terry, I told you two six-packs wouldn't be enough. You know being on the water makes me extra thirsty."

Terry says, "Screw you. You're always extra thirsty and damn near always complaining."

"Up yours. You sound just like …

"Yeah, yeah, I know. Just like your wife. Why don't you come up with a new line?"

The two men continue bickering. Ray has never known them just to talk—they argue about everything. When the three men were in school, they were constantly competing against each other. Eddie and Terry always disputed the results. If one voices an opinion, the other automatically takes a different side. Ray stays neutral, and Eddie and Terry admire his detachment. Their banter doesn't bother Ray, and he finds the men amusing—like the cartoon magpies Heckle and Jeckle.

Ray closes his mind to their chatter and looks over the lake. He likes the boat's easy rocking motion. Sitting still has never been easy, but since Peg left with their baby, movement of any kind always makes him feel calmer.

Ray sits low in the boat and studies the distant southwest shoreline—a faint irregular dark line between the gray-green water and the bright blue sky. Driven by a moderate breeze, large billowy clouds cast dark shadows over the boat, giving the men fleeting respite from the August sun. Sometimes the lake is calm, almost flat, but today the waves are about two feet high, steady and widespread. Ray enjoys being on the lake, but he especially likes it in storms and the waves rise to four or more feet.

While he lived in London, Ray had thought he would give up this crazy sport. But when he quit the job and moved back, he missed the lake could not resist buying this boat. Terry readily agreed to try their old game again, but they had to cajole Eddie to come on the lake with them. Ray can't help but think Eddie may be right about them being too old to be taking risks like this.

He swallows the last of his beer and holds the can below the water until it fills, then he opens his fingers and watches it disappear into the green depths. He tries calculating how long it will take the can to travel eighty feet to the bottom, but his thoughts shift to what the lake bottom looks like—all the cans and bottles and other stuff. It must be junky. People drown in the lake every year, and several of the bodies have never been found. He wonders how long it takes bodies to disintegrate.

A slight change in the air shakes his reverie. He sits up to pay attention to the moving clouds. He sniffs the air and searches the horizon, seeking signs of a storm. The wind is picking up, and the waves are growing larger. Ray knows storms come quickly on big lakes, and he can sense one in the distance. He enjoys being with his friends, but in a storm, he prefers to be alone.

He turns to his still-arguing friends and says, "You two do sound married. Let's get moving. I'm ready for another turn, and there's a storm on the way."

Eddie says, "Then it'll be time for some Wagon Wheel cheeseburgers and more beer."

Eddie and Terry finish their beers as Ray climbs over the windshield and scoots along the deck to the bow. He straddles the centerline dangling one leg on each side of the point. His weight lowers the bow and brings the cool water within inches of his knees. He takes the rope in his left hand and looks over his shoulder as the motor rumbles to life. In the driver's seat with one hand on the wheel and the other on the throttle, Terry waits for Ray's signal. Eddie, adjusting his life vest, sits to Terry's left. The rider and driver nod to each other, and Ray turns to face the oncoming water. Shifting to get himself over the centerline, he grips the rope, takes a deep breath, and signals Terry to go. Before his arm fully extends, the engine roars, the bow rises. The thrill is back.

Ray bought his boat for these moments. The salesman and the marina manager warned him that the engine was too large for the boat, but the risk motivated his purchase. Some people fish, some pull water skiers or make high-speed sightseeing trips, but Ray's boat, with its oversized motor, is to drive into and fight the waves. His friends worry and wear life vests. Despite their objections, Ray will not wear a vest.

Eddie and Terry have each ridden twice. Ray is on his sixth ride of the day. Since Peg left with the baby still in her womb and Jake died, he tells his friends this adrenaline rush is the best part of his life. He understands the potential deadliness of driving this boat in storms. He believes he isn't trying to kill himself but doesn't care if he does. He prefers being alone on the water, but he has more fun on the bow than in the boat. Ray doesn't want it to happen today and is glad Terry is driving. His stoic friend will accept whatever happens. If Eddie were at the wheel, he would feel guilty.

Terry drives into the wind. Under Ray's weight, water splashes up to the deck, and the bow rises slowly. He tightens his grasp on the rope. The wind-driven waves are nearly three feet high. Not huge, but they are growing, and the storm cloud is still miles away. Ray hears the motor change pitch and strain to push them forward. At the wave crest, the boat speeds full power to the bottom of the trough and plows into the next one. The force of the oncoming water smashes into Ray's body.

In the troughs, at least a half-mile from the nearest shore, water surrounds them, but on the wave crests, the storm cloud is visible on the horizon. Hanging on with both hands, Ray feels exhilaration charge through his body and brain each time the water hits him. They top a wave as lightning flashes in the distance. The boat slows, and he knows the water in the passenger compartment is too deep to keep going, and Eddie is unwilling to stay on the water when they see lightning.

Terry maneuvers the boat into a turn away from the wind and idles the engine. Ray releases the rope and slides over the rocking deck into the cockpit, and shouts, "God almighty, even bull riding can't be this much fun!"

"You are the craziest bastard I have ever known," Eddie says while he unscrews the drain cap.

"Maybe so, but I love it. Don't tell me you don't like it. You like it, don't you, Terry?"

"Hell yeah! I like it, but not the way you do—for once in his life, Eddie's right. You're crazy, and we're too old for this. How much longer you intend to keep it up?"

"Damned if I know. I think about it sometimes, but hitting that water makes me feel alive, really alive. I guess I keep doing it till Peg brings our son back. Or I no longer can."

ACT TWO

Our local theater group has performed two plays this season. They were great fun and box office successes, two necessary outcomes for amateur groups. But if the past hour is an indicator of the future, we may not do the third play.

Winston is our devoted and often overly enthusiastic director. His good friend Alan is our most creative member. Alan once worked, briefly, with a famous improv group in Chicago and made a pitch for our group to do a variation on improvisational theater. He and Winston have done this kind of thing before, and they made it sound like great fun. We agreed unanimously. Winston lauded us for the first unanimous vote since he founded the group.

The performance will not be actual improv. We will improvise and record three one-act plays. Alan will generate the scripts from the recorded rehearsals. The actual performance will be from Alan's script. The plan calls for us to record one act per night. Act One went beautifully last night. Act Two is still waiting to happen.

Earlier, we were chatting noisily about what Alan might have in mind for tonight. We were twenty minutes past start time when Winston, who has never been late, burst into the theater, shouting. "People! People! People! Stop! Stop! Stop!"

Like the well-disciplined troupe we are, the noise continued.

Winston cupped his hands, megaphone-like, "Quiet, please. Quiet." The noise dropped to a murmur, then died. We turned to face him. "Has anyone seen Alan? I've been waiting out front for him. We were supposed to meet at a quarter till."

Someone said, "He was in here at a quarter of seven. We said hello, but no sign of him since then." Another member said she also saw him earlier, but not lately. Others shook their heads.

Winston strode around the room, wringing his hands, "I simply don't know what to do. Alan is supposed to give us his thoughts on the scene he wrote for our starting point. Has anyone talked to him about the scene?"

Silence.

"Well, I'm not surprised. I'm his best friend, and he hasn't said a word to me. Who else would he tell?"

Winston frets as well as anyone I know. He looked at his watch, then at the door, at least three times in less than thirty seconds.

He faced us and said, "I don't see how, but we will have to start without him. Did everyone read the email he sent this morning?"

Winston looked at us, pausing on each face for just a moment, then he moaned and sagged.

"You didn't. Well, please listen closely. Here is what he gave us to set the beginning of the act."

Winston read aloud: "Albert is exhausted, but he keeps running. He stumbles over a rock in the trail and careens against a thorny bush. The barking grows louder."

"What are we doing? What is happening in this scene? Oh, why didn't I demand Alan ride with me tonight? Or at least explain what he was thinking?"

Silence.

"Charles, Albert will be your character. Why do you think he is running? Are the dogs chasing him, or does he think they are chasing him? If he thinks that, why? Has he seen the dogs? How big are they? Is Albert just clumsy, or is he startled, alarmed, frightened, terrified? Are they wild dogs? Did he encounter them when he went out for a stroll, or did someone set the dogs on him? Oh, my! Is it a pack of dogs, or just one? Alan? Alan!"

Winston paced about, looking at each entrance and exit—he looked everywhere except at the cast. "Where is Alan? Why is the playwright never around when I need him?"

Without slowing his pace or looking at us, he said, "Sallie, be a dear and search the building. Find Alan, will you, sweetheart. He must be somewhere in this old building crunching his creative mind about our project."

Winston did not notice that Sallie was not in the room or that no one had moved.

"I do wish that boy had set the scene before he abandoned us. This is so like him. All caught up in his creativity. He never gives a moment of thought to what I, his most devoted director, have to go through to translate his work for an audience.

"Does anyone have an idea what is going on? Where is Alan?

"Oooo, … I know—Albert did something naughty, and someone caught him doing it. Perhaps he was peeking in a window, and the dogs are guard dogs. But who was he peeking at and why? Is he a voyeur, a thief, an assassin?

"This is all so confusing. Why did I ever agree to do another improv play with that man? He is so frustrating, always coming up with scenes and never explaining what the hell got us to this place. This thing can go so many ways. Where is Alan? Why hasn't Sallie come back? God knows what she is doing to that poor boy. I should have sent someone else.

"George, please find them. Ooh, Ooh, Ooh, do be careful, dear. Don't just go around opening doors. Knock first. I don't want to embarrass Alan. It won't bother Sallie. She doesn't care who sees what. But Alan is so sensitive. If you embarrass him, he won't be able to work for at least a week. Then where will we be?

"Okay, people, take ten while George rescues me from this disaster. And please remember now, no smoking within fifty feet of the theater doors."

TIME GOES BY

O ld uncertainties about seeing classmates flared anew when Jennifer opened the 40th reunion notice. *Do I want to play that game? Am I really up to it?*

She remembers what she said to Avery after her 15th reunion. *Never again. Too much mommy-talk and too many paunchy former athletes reliving their few moments of glory.* When the 20th arrived, she said, *I'm not flying two thousand miles for a high school reunion.*

Jennifer shed tears as she read the invitation to her 25th. She and Avery were separated while she suffered through his temporary fascination with a younger, thinner woman.

She had no recollection of an announcement for her 30th reunion because she and Avery were vacationing in London. Her 35th happened the year Avery's boat exploded, the same year she learned she was asthmatic and admitted she was overweight.

It took months of persuasion and uncountable bottles of wine for Marion, her widowed sister, to persuade Jennifer to do something about her health and weight. Once convinced, she did both; and vowed not to waste the disciplined work she had put in to regain her health and figure. She promised herself. *I will have no more uncertainties. Get life going and have fun living it.*

Silently, she urged the airport escalator to move faster. Forty years since high school, and she felt great. All her friends said she looked beautiful. At the top of the escalator, she turned toward the gate. The last time she walked this concourse had been exhausting. But now, she knew she could do it without getting tired. Dr. Jones' diagnosis of asthma, the inhaler, plus a faithful diet and exercise regimen had turned her into a new woman. *Well, I did the turning. Jonesy and the inhaler made it possible.*

Jennifer smiled when she noticed a much younger man's eyes lingering on her. He smiled and winked. She knew she was strutting. *You got it again, kid. But these heels may be a bit much.*

She is excited about the trip. Having broken her depression from years of uncertainty over her rocky marriage, then her husband's death, she is determined to enjoy the rest of her life. She has only a slight interest in the reunion. She has rented a car and plans two weeks of carefree fun.

From the waiting area by the gate, she sees a tall, gray-haired uniformed man enter the gate area. *Can that really be him?* Her eyes follow as he approaches the desk. *It is him! Is he the pilot? Oh, my God! He is better-looking now than when we were in college. I have to say hello.*

"Thank you for your patience, ladies and gentlemen. In just a few minutes, we will begin boarding Flight 554 to Los Angeles." Jennifer sighed. *How could such a good-looking captain of my college football team wind up as a gate agent? Oh well, it doesn't matter. So damned handsome.*

She waits, wanting to be last in line. "Hello, Paul. So nice to see you after all these years. I hope you remember little Jennifer Palmer." The agent looked up, his expression blank behind his professional smile. Several long beats passed, he said, "Jennifer. Yes, it has been a long time."

She handed him her ticket, "You look wonderful, Paul. Goodness. I can't believe it's been so many years. How've you been?" His expression did not change, "Fine. I've been fine."

"I know you're busy now, but I'd love to talk about our college days together." She leaned close and whispered, "You used to be such a stud, Paul. I'm living in Roswell. I'm in the book—maiden name. Call me." Still smiling, he nodded slightly and handed her a boarding pass.

Mike's partner closes the gate behind Jennifer and grins at her co-worker. "Old girlfriend, Mike—oops, I mean Paul? Are you gonna call her?"

Mike shook his head. "My college roommate dated her a few times. Years and years ago."

"Why not call? So, what if she didn't remember your name. She remembered you were a stud."

Mike grins, "Always mixed me up with my roommate. Back then, she was a self-centered, teasing airhead. From what we just saw, I'm guessing she hasn't changed much."

Gazing aimlessly out the plane window, Jennifer sips her first wine of the day and thinks about Paul's reluctance to say he would call. She chuckles softly at an old memory. *I guess he may not be the stud he used to be back when he called me a stuck-up tease. But that's okay. I used to be a lot of things I'm not anymore.*

THERON'S BREAKFAST

Until a few years ago, I could still do most of the projects and repairs around the house. Lately, though, I have to rely more often on an expert, a handyman—especially when one of my do-it-myself projects goes wrong.

Theron is the handyman I depend on. He is an intelligent, competent man who has his own particular outlook on life. His father's family has been in this part of Georgia for generations, but Theron was the first in his family to go to college. After graduation from UGA, he got an excellent job with a bank. Theron says it took him five years to admit he was not cut out to work for other people and absolutely not in the city.

Since then, he has been an independent handyman and works on a schedule and terms he sets. He also provides unique insights about life as he sees it.

When the Occupy Wall Street protesters dominated the news, I asked Theron what he thought of the protests.

Continuing his work, Theron said. "Ought to vote."

I said, "Those folks believe the government and capitalism have failed them, and they are willing to get arrested or injured to make their point. What do you think about that?"

Theron said, "Don't."

I said, "But Theron, you know Americans have a history of protesting to change things. We had the Boston Tea Party and the civil rights sit-ins. Don't you believe in protests?"

Finally, he looked at me and said, "Believe they happen."

I asked, "What did you think of the demonstrations against the Vietnam War? Did you want to get drafted?"

Theron shook his head, "Joined the Army."

Because Theron has expressed bitterness about the Vietnam era, I assumed he had been drafted. "I didn't know you enlisted. Is there something else that would make you risk your life?"

He looked at me for a few seconds, shrugged, and made a mark on a board. When he finished cutting, he said, "Breakfast."

I said, "Did you say breakfast is worth risking your life?"

Theron said, "Breakfast is important. For me, it's gotta be eggs over-easy with sausage, grits, and Merita white bread toast. Then I want coffee with Carnation milk and two spoons of sugar."

I said, "That's not too hard to get."

Theron said, "My ex-wife didn't care for breakfast. Didn't matter to her one bit. One day she told me to fix it myself."

"Are you telling me you got a divorce because your wife wouldn't cook breakfast? Didn't you know how she felt before you two got married?"

He said, "Nowadays people live together before they get married. A man has a halfway decent chance of finding out before it's too late if a woman will fix breakfast. When we dated, she wouldn't even get in the back seat. Living together never crossed my mind, and I didn't know she didn't care for breakfast."

I said, "So now you cook your own breakfast?"

"For a long time after we split up, most mornings, I'd eat at the Waffle House. I like that place cause everyone who walks in gets a smile, and they say good morning. That makes me feel good."

My question had been about protests and risking injury. But in typical Theron fashion, we were on a different subject. So, I asked him if he would risk his life for breakfast.

After thinking a while, he said, "Well, there was one night, a bad ice storm was coming. I kept wakin' up worrying thinking I might slide off the road on the way to the Waffle House. At four o'clock, I got up and drove to breakfast. They said good morning and smiled just like they do when I get there at seven o'clock. Left those folks an extra big tip cause I knew it'd be a slow day."

I asked, "Would you risk getting arrested for breakfast?"

"One time when I was there, some punk started talking mean to his waitress and made me mad, so I went to his booth and whispered, real polite-like, that he better shut up and talk nice. And I told him what was gonna happen to him if he didn't."

I asked, "You whispered?"

"A couple of deputy sheriffs were there having breakfast. One of them is always looking for a reason to lock me up."

I asked, "Why would he do that?"

Theron said, "He's my ex-wife's brother."

I decided to go back into the house and leave Theron to his work. I turned to leave, but as I started up the steps, he said, "You know, though, there are two problems with the Waffle House."

There was no way I could walk away before finding out what those problems were. So, I asked him.

He said, "They don't make their toast with Merita bread, and they don't have Carnation milk for my coffee."

I said, "That's too bad, but nothing is perfect."

Theron shrugged, "It don't bother me a whole lot though."

The look on his face told me he wanted me to commiserate, so I said, "That's good. Breakfast is what counts, and I'm not sure I can tell one brand of canned milk from another."

For the first time in our conversation, I saw a slight upturn at one side of Theron's mouth. He said, "But I love it when the folks there always say hello. That's company policy. When the waitress serves my breakfast, that same policy says they have to say something nice. You know, like, 'Enjoy your breakfast.' Even though she's my ex-wife, and she don't care about breakfast."

OL' HANK, THE RABBIT

If you live around here, you know we have a new diner in town. Well, it is not exactly new. It has been open a while, but trying unfamiliar restaurants, is not one of my pleasures. I heard enough folks say the food is good, so last week, I tried it myself. Approaching the door, I chanced to meet my handyman.

We see each other mostly when Theron is working at my house. I welcome every opportunity to talk with him, and I was delighted he accepted my invitation to eat lunch together. He is an educated and observant man who chooses to be a self-employed handyman. He is good company and will talk about an issue and not touch on party politics, although sometimes he will voice a strong opinion regarding an individual politician.

We studied the menu in silence—an easy thing to do because Theron is not overly talkative. It may not matter to anyone except me, but we both ordered the meatloaf sandwich. While we waited, Theron inquired about my writers' group, as he does that almost every time I see him.

At the group's most recent meeting, we each described a frightening personal experience. Theron listened without commenting as I listed some of the examples.

Then he said, "Fright means different things to different folks."

"Yes," I said, "and we heard several different meanings."

I've known Theron for a while now, and we have become friends. Around me, he has dropped almost all of his country-boy way of talking and speaks more like the well-educated, intelligent man he is.

When the server delivered our food, Theron wasted no time with preliminaries; he was chewing his first bite before the warm meaty aroma had fully engaged my sense of smell. The generously buttered, grilled sourdough bread first concealed and then enhanced the burst of taste waiting inside. The flavor was smooth, spicy, and delicious. After a couple of bites, Theron and I agreed we had made the right choice.

Theron studied his sandwich as though deciding where to bite next. I said, "How do you define frightening?"

He lifted one eyebrow and said, "War." He bit the sandwich and chewed in silence, then sipped his coffee. "This really is good. Spicier than the meatloaf sandwiches I usually eat."

I chewed, managed to mumble an uh-huh, and then kept quiet. Experience told me Theron had more to say.

He almost finished the first half of his sandwich before he said, "Fright is complex. A one-word definition doesn't do it justice. Not everybody goes to war, but everybody does get frightened. To me, it means terrifying. A lot more than startling or just causing your heart to race. A frightening experience makes reactions instinctive and rational thoughts difficult, maybe impossible." He took a bite of pickle.

I said, "That's a good definition."

Our server refilled our drinks and asked if we wanted anything more. Theron laughed and said, "Check back in a few minutes. That coconut pie is calling me, and I need to think about what my answer is gonna be."

I took that to mean he had more to say, so I asked, "Other than combat, have you ever had a terrifying experience?"

"A near-miss car wreck, but that happened so fast there was no time to be frightened. But, realizing what almost happened set me shaking. Had to stop the car to get control of myself." He paused and then said, "Since Nam, I've led a quiet life."

"How about when you were a kid? Every kid gets frightened."

Theron's face can be as expressionless as any I have ever seen. I assumed he was pondering my question, but the long silence made me wonder if he had heard my question. Then a barely perceptible upward twitch in one corner of his mouth flickered to the other corner. He said, "Until third grade, I was afraid of fistfights. But my brother Dewey got me over it. Have I told you about Dewey?"

"No, but I'd like to know more."

"Well, we never knew if Dewey loved drinking more than fighting or fighting more than drinking. But he was a good brother, and he taught me to defend myself. Someday, I'll tell you some stories, but not now. We're talking about fright. By fifth grade, I was a pretty brave kid. Then an angry rabbit showed up."

Theron nibbled at his chips, savoring them like they were the best chips ever served.

I'm not known for my restraint, but I waited until curiosity got the better of me. "A rabbit?"

Theron nodded, "I knew a lot about rabbits. When I was five or six, my grandfather started taking me rabbit and squirrel hunting, and I got to be a good hunter. But my real lessons on rabbits came from helping a neighbor who raised them."

Theron can be maddening sometimes. I sipped my tea and waited to see how long it would take for him to get around to the angry rabbit story I knew he would tell.

In less time than I expected, Theron continued.

"Our next-door neighbors had a rabbit hutch in their back yard. I helped feed them. I took a shine to a big, orange-colored buck, and I named him Hank, even though Pop had made it plain that the rabbits were being raised for meat, not as pets. Naming that rabbit was not the smartest thing I ever did."

By this time, I was wondering where Theron was going with the story. We started out talking about fright, and he was acting dreamy over a rabbit named Hank. I said, "Naming a rabbit can't be so bad. Lots of kids name animals they know will wind up on somebody's dinner table."

"That's true," Theron said. "I knew ol' Hank would end up in the pot, but I talked to him like some folks talk to their dogs. I swear he responded when I called his name."

The server interrupted, and Theron ordered pie and more coffee. I settled for more tea.

"The rabbit pens were not very big, so one day, I took ol' Hank out of his pen to let him enjoy the grass. You remember how boys are. Never even think about what might happen. Only what seems worth doing right at the moment."

I nodded, remembering my serious lack of judgment when I was a boy. Not that it got measurably better with age.

Theron chuckled, "Well, ol' Hank liked the grass, but when it came time to put him back in the hutch, he hopped away. The more I tried to catch him, the faster and farther away he hopped. He didn't even pause when I called his name."

"How big was the yard?"

"They had farmland, and a rabbit hutch was in a fenced yard behind the house. Catching a rabbit in a fenced backyard ought to be easy for a twelve-year-old boy, but it ain't. I finally got ol' Hank into a corner, and he had no way to go except toward me. He didn't look panicked or anything. He looked just like he always did when I fed and petted him. But when I reached to pick him up, he changed into something I had never seen before."

Theron leaned toward me and lowered his voice as though he did not want other people to hear him. He said, "Ol' Hank got his back against that fence, his back paws came up off the ground. Toenails sticking out like claws. Big ol' rabbit teeth bared and looking bigger than his head. I reached for him one more time, and he screamed—a blood-curdling, loud, hissing, angry noise. I didn't know rabbits screamed. The sound cut right through me."

Theron paused, but I could see he was thinking. He leaned back, "Have you ever heard a rabbit scream?"

"No, but I'd like to, just not under those circumstances. What did you do then?"

"I got away from there quick, but our neighbor was coming out of her house. I think she laughed, but that memory has faded into the oblivion it deserves. As far as I know, ol' Hank is still in the corner of her yard, but most likely, he became rabbit stew."

I said, "Well, it doesn't sound so scary at my age now, but it sure would have been back then."

With a slight backhanded dismissive wave, he said, "Oh yeah, Hank made my pulse race. But so many strange things went on in that neighborhood I forgot it. I don't remember even thinking any more about it until the great swamp rabbit attack of 1979."

"The great what?"

Theron smiled. "Don't you remember the headlines? The one I liked best said, 'Jimmy Carter attacked by Killer Rabbit.'"

I laughed. "I think the entire world was smirking."

"Well, I wasn't," Theron said. "I had never heard of swimming rabbits, but the story about the rabbit attacking the president while he was fishing rang true with me. All I could see was ol' Hank's claws and teeth right there in front of me. His scream shooting right through me all over again." Theron paused and leaned back before saying, "I was terrified." He fell silent, gazing into the distance.

I tried to be respectful and waited a few seconds before saying, "Memory can do bizarre things, Theron. Bringing back a frightening experience is not unusual."

He snapped his eyes back toward me and said, "The memory wasn't what terrified me. It was realizing that I had something in common with Jimmy Carter."

DINNER WITH THERON

Last week, Theron came to silence a squeaky floorboard and correct some of the other problems our old house seems to keep developing. He wasn't here more than five minutes when he said, "Has Mrs. R. been away long?" Theron is as observant as he is curious. To him, it was apparent I had been alone for a few days.

"She's at a reunion with her sorority sisters. It's nice she can have time with them. Seeing old friends always gives me a feeling of continuity in life."

Theron said, "How do you like cooking for yourself?"

"What is there to like? Cereal for breakfast, except today I ate at the Bread & Bacon Barn for a bacon biscuit. Soup or a sandwich for lunch. Dinner is easy. Microwave some mac 'n' cheese or a pot pie. A glass of beer or wine helps dinner settle just fine."

"I just thought you might be missing her cooking. You've talked about what a great cook she is."

Theron turned and walked out to his truck. I'm not sure what he does there, but like most other people who come here to work, Theron always makes one or two trips to his vehicle. When I walk my dogs, I sometimes see repairmen and contractors sitting in their trucks talking on a cell phone. It's not my business, so I try to ignore it. I went back to work on my great American novel—mostly to stay out of Theron's way when he came back.

When I handed him the check for his work, Theron said, "Tomorrow, I'm gonna cook a couple of Angus steaks I get from a friend. I'd like it if you would join in. My wife's gone to a horse show and won't be back till Monday. Besides, Lucy hardly eats enough steak to matter, so she won't mind if you get one. Just be us. We can do a little fishing in my pond. I'm not much of a cook, except for steaks on a wood fire. Besides, I hope you'll tell me about that book you're writing."

He didn't know it unless my wife had told him, but Theron struck a bullseye with that offer, and I said yes. He drew me a map and told me not to bother with equipment because he had a slew of tackle and different baits.

Let me set the record straight on a couple of things. I miss my wife. And I tend to skip shaving and washing dishes while she is away. But it never occurred to me that those things, which I assume all men do when they are alone, would make me look like I needed company. Although his invitation pleased me, it came as a surprise. Theron and I shared lunch once at the local diner when he told me about his adventure with Hank, the rabbit, but it hadn't occurred to me he would want me to come to his house.

Theron is excellent company, and he has mentioned his farm a few times before. It sounded idyllic, too tempting to resist, so I said, "I'd be honored to come as long as you promise not to serve rabbit." He laughed and promised he wouldn't.

When I turned into his driveway, the sun had settled low enough to produce highlights and shadows on the mountainside. His brick ranch-style house was set far back from the road and nestled in a small grove of oaks, still clinging to their last brown leaves. The air was late-autumn crisp and fresh smelling but with hints of horse manure. I won't tell you where Theron lives, except that his home is north of here and the view from his patio to the mountains is across a big Bermuda grass lawn sloping to a farm pond he said was ten or so acres. Three happy, tail-wagging dogs, including one with only three legs, accompanied us on a brief tour of the house and barn and outbuildings. Those dogs responded to Theron as though they were extensions of the man.

"Those dogs certainly are well behaved," I said.

"Grandpa raised dogs. You ain't seen nothing till you've seen him put a pack through their paces. Hunting dogs, show dogs, even garden-variety mutts. Papa did it all. And, man, did those dogs love pleasing him. I'm lucky he shared a bit of his talent with me, but you should see these critters with Lucy."

The dry grass crunched under our feet as we walked to the pond. The fishing was fun, and it didn't matter that it wasn't highly productive. The company was downright pleasant. I don't recall meeting more than a couple of people as relaxed and comfortable with themselves as my host.

It was dark when Theron cooked the steaks over hardwood in the firepit next to his patio. We were camping with all the conveniences of home. As we ate, I told him about my novel. He said it sounded complicated. Honestly, I agreed with him. The story had become so complex and bogged down I couldn't figure out what to do next.

I asked about his life before he had become a handyman. I knew he worked for a bank, but that's all. He poured bourbons for us, and said, "Wasn't much to it. I grew up in this house. Pop's family settled here a long time ago, but succeeding generations drifted away and sold it all except for these couple hundred acres. After high school, I got married like most all the other kids. That didn't work out. I had a bad need for adventure and joined the Army and was lucky enough to live through a tour in Nam. When that was over, I studied finance at UGA. That's where I met Lucy."

The dogs were running and wrestling by and in the pond. Bobby, a three-legged border collie-whippet mix, wrestled and swam right in there with the much larger black Lab and golden retriever. When Theron tossed more wood on the fire, the dogs shook themselves, trotted up the slope, and settled on the patio.

"We moved down close to Atlanta. The promotions started coming, and I was even thinking about moving to New York. Pop's bachelor brother, Dewey, died, and a few months later, Pop passed on, and I inherited this place."

As he talked, Theron tossed a steak scrap toward Bobby. It arced through the faint light, and the dog lifted his head and snatched it. The other dogs did not move.

"We put it on the market because there was no time to tend to it. But as soon as I signed the listing agreement, I realized the job was killing me—wearing me out. I'm too much a loner. Introverted is what Lucy says is my problem."

He tossed another piece of steak, higher this time. Bobby rose on his one back leg, caught it, and curled up beside the other dogs. He was graceful and quick and appeared to exert no effort except to keep his eyes on Theron. The other two dogs didn't move.

"To make it short, we sold the house in Atlanta, took the profit, and came back here to be my own boss and live life at my own pace, not under some city boy who wouldn't know a horse's dong from a cow's udder. Lucy's happy working with horses, and she always loved this place."

He picked up a steak bone in each hand, and the two big dogs were immediately sitting side-by-side in front of him. He gave them the bones, and they moved off the patio to gnaw privately. Bobby didn't lift an eyebrow. But when Theron underhanded a scrap high into the air, Bobby jumped at least his own height with his mouth open and caught it.

I could not be quiet any longer and complimented Theron's dog training one more time. He credited his grandfather.

"Papa had two tripod dogs. One lost a leg in a trap. A cow stepped on the other one. The owners were gonna shoot 'em, but Papa took 'em to train and entertain his grandkids. He taught me to work with dogs. They always amaze me that they are so smart and want to please people."

He tossed more wood on the fire, and sparks rose into the night. Before they settled, a sudden breeze pushed them out toward the pond. Theron stood silently, watching them drift down toward the dry grass. When he was satisfied, he patted Bobby on the head and said something I did not catch, but it sounded like "fire watch." Bobby licked his hand.

We settled back with our bourbon, enjoying the cool night air and country quiet. Suddenly, Theron said, "Bobby! Fire!" and threw a steak scrap really high.

The dog leaped off the patio running toward two small blazes in the Bermuda between us and the pond. At the closer blaze, he lifted a leg and peed on it, then sped to extinguish the other one. He got back to us and snatched that steak before it hit the ground.

I was babbling on and on about Bobby's speed and agility until Theron said, "Before he lost that leg, Bobby could piss on three or four and still catch his treat. I reckon he does all right for a three-legged mongrel, but he used to be a real pisser."

EULOGY FOR PELZER EASLEY

Theron continues to amaze me with his diverse talents, but the intriguing people I have met through him cause me to believe his past life was not as uninteresting as he claims. One example is Hershel Moore, and through him, Pelzer Easley—although I didn't meet Mr. Easley because he was already dead when I first heard of him.

Theron invited me to go with him to a memorial celebration for Pelzer Easley, an elderly black man who had been particularly important to Theron and was loved by almost everybody in the town. It wasn't a church service and would be in the high school auditorium. A longtime friend was to deliver a eulogy, and Theron wanted me to hear it.

I hesitated, but Theron described the ribs at the barbeque joint where he wanted us to eat lunch. Of course, I agreed to go. Theron knows his ribs and pulled pork. Then he said, "I'd appreciate it if you'd use your phone and video the eulogy. I want to share it with an old pal who can't travel anymore."

We had heard several short tributes when Theron said, "My friend Hershel is next. He's the one I'd like for you to record." I did make the video, and I'm glad Theron invited me. The following is my transcription of Hershel Moore's eulogy for Pelzer Easley.

Alice, thank you for inviting me to say a few words in tribute to your father. Pelzer Easley was the best friend I've ever had. The best friend anyone could ever dream of having.

Mr. Easley lived in the same place for all of his ninety-four years, and I'd bet that everyone here has a positive Pelzer Easley story. I would be genuinely surprised to learn that even a hint of negative has ever been connected with his name. But no one knows all the good he did for the people in his community. Memorial services allow us to learn something we did not know about the person we gather to honor. Today, I have learned Pelzer cut and hauled firewood to folks who could not do it themselves. I often saw his garden, but I wasn't aware he tended and gave the products of three gardens to others.

I want to share something, I think, none of you know.

We are here to honor Pelzer Easley, but I have to tell you a little about my mama to clarify how important Pel was to me. The summer I met Mr. Easley, my life had gone from wonderful to bad to awful. But thanks to him, it started back toward good.

A few of y'all remember my mama. When I was twelve, she and Pastor Jenkins got me stirred up about being saved, becoming a Christian, and joining the church. Well, I did, and that made Mama joyous and Pastor Jenkins happy. He told me the Lord was pleased, and I believed life was as it ought to be.

We were all happy for a little more than a year. Then Mama went to the hospital and was diagnosed with cancer. Well, she didn't look sick, and she acted like everything would be all right. It didn't sink in with me just how ill she was.

When she passed on, I was one incredibly sad little boy. I was ready to die myself. All I could do was cry and think how lonesome I was. Daddy was dead, and now Mama had died. It was just me and my brother Aaron. I didn't believe for one minute that Aaron would have time for me. He had a girlfriend, and they were planning to get married.

I was so miserable I just stayed home. I didn't go to school or take care of myself. I started thinking I should just jump off the bridge and let Cypress Creek wash me down to the river and into the Gulf. One day I wrote a note for Aaron and headed to the bridge. I was walking along the creek bank and thinking it was time to die when someone whispered, "Quit walkin' Herschel. Don't scare 'im off."

I looked up, and there stood Pelzer Easley. "Scare who?"

He put his fingers up to his lips and shushed me. He pointed across the creek, "That scarlet tanager. You see 'im?"

And sure enough, at the edge of the water was the brightest little red bird I had ever seen. I still don't know why, but I stood there real quiet. We watched that bird till he flew away. Then he asked me if I had ever seen such a pretty bird.

I spent the rest of the afternoon listening to him. He didn't mention Mama or school. He talked about birds, how they build nests, and how short their lives are. He told me some of the terrible things that happen to birds, including the creatures that eat them, things that make them get sick and die and how little boys and men kill them for fun.

The next day I met Pel at the same spot and brought my fishing pole as he told me. I don't remember catching anything, but I sure learned a lot about fish and fishing. That man knew even more fish facts and stories than he did about birds.

That was a whole lotta years ago, but from the time Mama passed until I graduated from high school, I spent my spare time with Pelzer Easley. He wasn't Ol' Pel then. I'm guessing he must have been between forty to fifty when he saved my life and became my best friend.

But Pelzer Easley did more than save my life; he shaped it and helped me get enthusiastic about living. It wasn't easy for him to do either. But he took a suicidal little boy and made him forget jumping off that bridge.

I knew his name that day on the creek, but I knew nothing about him. In those days, white boys didn't bother getting to know black men. Honestly, it had never occurred to me to get to know

Pel or any other black folks in town. I just lived my life and never thought to look beyond it.

Pelzer Easley changed that, and he changed me.

I learned something new on every one of those days I spent with him. He never went to school, but he was knowledgeable, and he understood the importance of education. He got me interested in studying my school lessons. He convinced me to go to college. I didn't see the need to do either. I wanted to work outdoors with birds, animals, and fish. The way I saw it, Pelzer knew everything I needed to know.

But he said, "Herschel, I know enough to get by around here and do what I do. But that ain't near enough." He convinced me there was a lot he didn't know. Not like some folks, he understood he didn't know everything.

I am blessed to have known Mr. Easley. When I got through college, I came back here to live and teach biology. Many of you know he was a frequent guest in my classes. He enjoyed talking about wildlife and plants, and his way of doing it made students want to learn more.

If you were fortunate enough to have taken my biology class, you had the opportunity to hear him, and you know Pelzer Easley was a gifted teacher.

I look out at this congregation—at his family and friends gathered to pay respects to a wonderful man—and I feel joy. Yes, we are sad Pelzer is no longer gracing us with his little off-center smile and no longer doing all the things that made him dear to us. But the joy is genuine. We know Pelzer loved us, and who could ask for more on this Earth.

Pelzer Easley. A man who didn't let the injustices he suffered because of his skin color keep him from helping another human being. He knew I was hurting when he stopped me that day on the creek bank, but he didn't say so. He just helped me.

As far as I know, Pelzer never asked anybody for anything. He spent his life working odd jobs for the white folks who would hire him for a few hours or a few days. I never heard him complain—not once. Shoot! He was so good-natured he didn't even complain about the weather.

Times have changed since my days with Pelzer Easley on the banks of Cypress Creek. He knew how the world was supposed to be, and he did all he could to help make it better. I look around this church, and I see many folks who have learned something from him. Although I don't know each of you, I know that your presence here today means you have benefited from his attempts to make our world better—one deed at a time. Now he's gone. There is no doubt in my mind all the souls in heaven are rejoicing he has joined them.

I hope none of us will ever forget what he taught us about how to live in a community. There is no more fitting way to pay tribute to Pelzer Easley than to live the lessons he taught and pass them along to others.

Scarlet tanagers have been special to me since the day Pelzer Easley saved my life and became my friend. I am grateful for his teachings, but most of all, I am thankful for his sense of belonging to a community and his willingness to help others through difficult times in their lives. Thank you, Mr. Easley

TRESPASSERS WILL BE SHOT

Winter in our mountains has been long, wet and icy. I did not leave the house for one eight-day period except to walk our dogs. When, at last, we had a relatively warm, ice-free day, I went out to get a haircut and run errands. Marty also told me it was time for her to have the house to herself.

I was a couple of weeks overdue for a haircut when the storm arrived, and Albert, my barber, needed longer than usual to deal with the extra shag. He is a quiet barber, and he never mentioned the length of my hair. I prefer quiet, but on that day, I needed to hear voices other than my wife's—human voices, not TV voices.

I walked a couple of blocks to a popular lunch place. Outside the restaurant, I saw Theron, my handyman, talking with a slender, hawk-nosed fellow I did not know. Not wanting to interrupt what might be business, I reached for the restaurant door, and Theron called my name.

"Mr. R. Come on over. I want you to meet my friend Crews Dillingham." The invitation brought a rush of pleasure. Eight days of isolation was about to end.

Theron has never struck me as gregarious, and I have described him as taciturn. Although he usually has a good tale to share when he straightens out my failed do-it-myself projects. I've only met a few of his friends and the ones I've met are intriguing. As we exchanged pleasantries, I admired Crews' mellow baritone—he would have made an excellent old-time radio announcer.

Unable to curb my curiosity, I said, "Crews Dillingham is really an intriguing name. Do you mind if I ask how you came by it?"

Theron's startled wide-eyed expression made me suspect I had made a mistake. Before Crews could answer, he said, "Hey, I hate to run, but I need to see a customer. I'll leave you two to talk. Anyway, I already know how this old boy got his name."

Crews raised his hand to acknowledge Theron and said, "I don't mind you asking. It's a family story if you're interested."

"Oh, I'm interested." But I had thought my question was only small talk. Crews, on the other hand, took my interest seriously. For the next twenty minutes, he alternated between boring me and fascinating me with his account of his convoluted family history.

He leaned against a street lamppost and said, "I just say that Crews is a family name, and I never thought much about it until a while back when me and Sarah Anne were watching the news about that plane crash, the one that killed Senator Ted Stevens from Alaska. The announcer summarized the rescue efforts, and he said, 'Crews spent the night in Dillingham.'

"Sarah Anne laughed. I asked what was funny, and she said, 'Crews spent the night in Dillingham,' and that's you, Crews Dillingham. She thought it was funny, but I didn't, and I reminded her we live in Georgia, not Alaska.

"Then Sarah Anne said she liked my name, Crews Matthews Dillingham, and she knows Matthews was my mother's maiden name, but not why Mama named me Crews.

"I didn't remember why, and so Sarah Anne told me to call Mama, so I did.

"Mama told me it bothers her, and she sometimes wonders why I had so little interest in my distinguished pedigree. Then, she asked me why it took me so long to inquire. I laughed, but not aloud because that would have made Mama mad as hell. I remembered Daddy always said Mama would use a ten-cent word where a nickel one would do every time.

"I told her what we heard on TV. She thought it was funny too. Then she said my not remembering who she named me for was disappointing because I had heard it before, and if I had forgotten my namesake, it did not show much pride to wait till she was an old woman and almost dead before I asked about it. For the millionth time, she told me I should be proud of my heritage.

"I took the phone away from my ear and looked at Sarah Anne and made like my hand was talking-talking-talking. I do that every time I talk on the phone with Mama."

Crews made the gesture, and I thought it applied to him also.

He continued, "Mama was going on about heritage. She talked a lot about it when I was a little boy, but she stopped mentioning it almost entirely after Daddy died. Then I got married and moved to Macon and didn't see her very much anymore, so she went to Florida to live with her sister, my aunt.

"Finally, she reminded me that she named me after her great-granddaddy, whose name was Crews Sutcliffe Matthews. And once more, she reminded me Matthews was her maiden name, and her great-granddaddy was my great-great-granddaddy.

"To tell the truth, Mama always was just a little bit on the snobby side. Daddy said so more than she liked, but she said she couldn't help herself cause her mama taught her to be that way.

"Mama said her granddaddy, Harold Sutcliffe Matthews, had lived in Chapman, Georgia when he was little, and her great-granddaddy, Crews Sutcliffe, owned timberland and sawmills and a railroad to haul lumber to Savannah. She didn't know where her great-granddaddy Sutcliffe was born because somebody shot him after he was mayor and was about to become a congressman. Her granddaddy was twelve when somebody shot his daddy, and he had never asked where his daddy was born.

"When his daddy got shot, his mother died of a broken heart, and the bank took everything. So, all by themselves, Harold and his brother, Walter, went to Texas to live with an uncle, but Walter kept on going to California.

"Well, Mama took a lot longer time to tell the story than it's taking me to tell it to you. I told Sarah Anne what Mama had said about my name, and she said that her mother knew some genealogy. Well, they convinced me to try to find out where my great-great-granddaddy was born by looking at the census.

"I decided to try and find out because I wanted to do something nice for Mama."

By then, I understood why Theron had left in such a hurry. Crews talked nonstop and he hadn't moved from the lamppost or altered his delivery pace. The man hardly had drawn a breath.

"The census was interesting, but the only Matthews in Chapman had a boy named Thomas. I told Sarah Anne we were wasting time. She showed me that listed right under the Matthews family was a family named Sutcliffe, with two boys named Harold and Walter, and were the same ages as Mama's granddaddy Harold and his brother Walter. Their daddy's name was Herman Sutcliffe.

"Well, I told Sarah Anne we were at a dead end. She argued we ought to go to Chapman and find out where my great-great-granddaddy, Crews, was born because not knowing would always bother me. I guessed she was right because it had been bothering me for almost a month already when we checked the census."

Crews didn't seem to notice when a truck with a busted muffler roared to life in the parking space next to us. He didn't change his position or his volume. And he continued talking.

"We went to the library in Chapman and looked for the newspapers from when my great-granddaddy was twelve years old. They had a newspaper because Chapman was a lot bigger back then, but it was just a weekly. We couldn't find a death notice for Crews Matthews.

"The disappointment made me want to have a drink, but Sarah Anne said back then sometimes people got their ages mixed up, and Mama's granddaddy might have been born in a different year. So, we looked in the papers for the year before Mama thought her granddaddy was twelve. We were into October when we saw a headline that said, 'Local Man Shot Stealing Chickens.'"

Crews stood away from the lamp and quoted the headline, making those wiggly signs people use to represent quote marks. I can only describe his grin as impish. Before I could say a word, he eased back against the lamppost and continued talking.

"Well, that surprised me, and I laughed out loud, but Sarah Anne made me promise never to let Mama know what we found. It is okay for me to tell the story now because Mama was old then, and she died a few months after we discovered that the man Mama named me after—Crews Sutcliffe Matthews—was really named Herman Sutcliffe, and the only accurate part of her story was my great-great-granddaddy died of a gunshot.

"The newspaper story told how a local farmer caught a man stealing chickens and shot him, but he didn't know it was Herman Sutcliffe. It was the third time somebody stole chickens from him. The sheriff said a man had a right to protect his property, and his chicken house had a big warning saying trespassers will be shot."

Crews leaned toward me and said, "I just love telling the next part of the story, especially when Theron is around." He leaned back against the lamppost and continued.

"The newspaper said Herman Sutcliffe was a popular local character who everybody knew as 'Crews' because he was a general handyman and fixer-upper who always boasted he could get a crew to take care of any job that folks needed done.

"According to the paper, the mayor said that Chapman would miss Crews because he was an excellent handyman, and they are hard to find. It is sadder that Crews had been shot stealing chickens leaving behind his wife and two sons.

"The next week's paper said Crews Sutcliffe's widow collapsed when she heard her husband had been shot, and she died the next day. Then it said the widow's brother, and next-door neighbor, was a carpenter named James Matthews. The brother said he had planned to go to Texas but had put it off because his sister had a weak heart. Since the trouble happened, he did not have a reason to stay, and he planned to head that way soon and take his sister's two boys with him as his own.

"It would have killed Mama if I told her my great-great-granddaddy was a chicken thief. I'm truly sorry she was wrong about it, but once in a while, things can be sad and funny at the same time.

"Used to be when folks asked me about my name, I'd say it's a family name. Now I can say my namesake was a railroad baron, a lumber tycoon, and a politician who was also a chicken thief."

I escaped from Crews, skipped lunch, and headed to the library. More than food, I needed a quiet place with no human voices. I also wanted to think of a new project for Theron. Right now, adding flooring in my unfinished attic in July sounds about right. He deserves to know how much I appreciate him introducing me to his friend Crews Dillingham.

BESMIRCHED

Weldon does not want Claudia to know he is attracted to her. He avoids making eye contact, but he secretly watches her flirt, laugh, sigh, and tease as she moves from one booth to the next. For the twentieth or thirtieth time, he tells himself the woman is not pretty. This creature is not for me. He sure as hell doesn't want his friends to know he wants her. Smirching his reputation over a waitress who flirts with every male and some of the female customers would be unbearable.

Weldon has no problem getting dates since he matured from a gawky, unsure kid into a tall, handsome, easy-going guy. Women encourage him, even ask him for dates. Every hostess has his name on her guest list, he is an eligible bachelor, and he never talks about himself. His male friends envy his successes at work and with the women they believe he seduces.

He is proud of his reputation, but he is aware that his pride makes him unable to repress memories of his mother's nagging about the importance of other people's opinions. His mother died five years ago, and he thought he was over her. Then Claudia came to work at Dusty's Place, his favorite watering hole, where Weldon's friends regularly gather at the end of the week. Some are single, some married. Claudia flirts and teases indiscriminately. She chooses partners on her terms—at least, that is what Weldon and his friends believe. No one seems to know for sure if she selects anyone. That he even thinks of risking his status to chase a waitress like Claudia disturbs Weldon's self-assurance.

Claudia knows her face is plain, and her body is zaftig. Her mother taught her to flirt and use the power of her body, and an older waitress on her first job trained her to be an excellent waitress. She is grateful to both women and uses the skills to tease and flirt while working hard. She learned early that the combination keeps men ogling and tipping.

Although the work is hard, and too many customers are rude and demanding, she enjoys the job. She needs the tips and takes none of the teasing interplay seriously. But she is young and sometimes chooses a sex partner from among her customers. She picked Weldon on her first night at Dusty's. She knows he watches and is bewildered that he avoids looking directly at her.

Weldon did not have a sex partner until after his mother died and his fear of displeasing her ceased to worry him. Since then, he cannot get enough. At first, he suspected something might be physically wrong, but he liked being able to go on and on. His shyness disappeared, and now he treasures having women phone to tell him they have heard.

He does not want to lose that pleasure, and the thought of losing his reputation among his friends terrifies him. He believes pursuing Claudia will destroy it. When dreams of untying her uniform top disturb his sleep, he tells himself he has plenty of beautiful partners. Why bother with this—waitress? But alone in bed, neither his mind nor his body will not cooperate.

Claudia has not figured out why Weldon hasn't pursued her. She sees him as a trophy she intends to win and has waited for him to make a move, but his only response has been those furtive glances. It is time to take the situation in hand.

The place is crowded, and twice, Claudia crosses in front of Weldon as he waits in line to pay his tab. He struggles not to look and focuses on the head before him when her hand touches his stiffening penis as she whispers, "Just as I suspected, a semi-hard." That night, and for many more nights, Weldon does not sleep well.

The discomfort rises several times every day. She pops into his mind in all kinds of places—the shower, at breakfast, in meetings, and as he walks to lunch alone. *I will not call her. I do not want her.* The worst times come in the pre-dawn hours when he begins to awaken and dreams of Claudia's cleavage, her fleeting, gentle touch. Later, with his discomfort temporarily eased, he tries to recall details from a long-ago psychology lecture on understanding the difference between wanting and needing.

WACKO AND LITTLE EDDY

Larry savored the grits. For a roadhouse, they were terrific, just enough black pepper and Tabasco. Roberta would not be happy. She always whined when he added Tabasco to his food, claimed she could taste it on his lips for two days. But what the hell! Roberta was never happy except when sipping Mojitos on a beach.

The fiery pepper sauce made Larry's face flush red. He knew it would, but he added it anyway. He loved the stuff. He was tugging at the ill-fitting collar of his dress shirt when he saw the pink Mustang with a green iguana on the door pull into the parking lot.

A tall, spectacularly proportioned woman with orange hair stepped from the driver's seat, and Larry's gut clenched. *Damn, wouldn't you know. And me in a hurry to get south.* Between the same-pink-as-the-Mustang skinny jeans and cropped top, a green tattoo shouted from her bare belly. With her back turned toward the cafe, she stretched and bent to touch her feet reminding Larry of Roberta's fondness for the downward dog yoga pose. Then, like a model on a catwalk, she strutted toward the entrance.

Larry stays alert to the possibility of fresh action, but today though, he has to get back on the road and deal with Poppy's job. When he saw the orange hair enter his section of the cafe, he averted his eyes to stare at the label on the Tabasco bottle. *Look anywhere but at that fantastic body.* He pressed fingers against his temples and didn't notice the woman pause a couple of booths before his. He thought about Roberta and what she had told him two days ago.

She has her way of making life wonderful and miserable at the same time, and he couldn't shake the memory of their last conversation. He sat on the edge of the bed, relishing the afterglow of lovemaking. Roberta's eyes invited him to lie back down, but her voice said, "You should be smart and take Poppy's offer. It's worth fifty, maybe sixty grand."

Larry refused to rise to either bait. "Jimmy said seventy-five is not nearly enough for what Poppy wants."

Roberta laughed, "Jimmy doesn't worry about money." She rolled to the far side of the bed and stood, crushed her cigarette into the ashtray, and said, "I gotta get going. You don't mind, do you, Larry? Billy resisted the idea of me meeting you, and I don't want to get him agitated again."

Larry had lost interest in the Tabasco label and was staring at the ketchup label when he sensed someone at his booth. Knowing it would be her, he turned to face a one-eyed green iguana, only the eye was her navel. He raised his gaze to her smile.

"Do you like Little Eddy?"

"Your iguana is named Little Eddy?"

"He's named after Big Eddy, the first person I met when I got into the business. He was a real lizard, but he did a lot for me. When he got his reward, I vowed never to forget what he did for me, or to me."

Orange hair, violet eyes, and a green lizard on her belly. Larry didn't want to ask what business she was in, but he suspected and also suspected he knew what Eddy had done to her. He liked to move fast in the morning and needed to get on the road, but he couldn't take his eyes off this incredible woman delaying him. He said, "You mean Big Eddy Culloch from Dean's Blue Hole?"

"The same. Did you know him?"

"What do you mean, did?"

"He got dropped off in a stone lighthouse on an island in Lake Erie in the winter. Left him a few jugs of water and tins of food, but that couldn't have helped much. No way to build a fire. It's some kind of a bird place, so nobody goes there much. I almost felt sorry for the son-of-a-bitch. So how did you know Big Eddy."

Larry was confused. He didn't know this woman, and she had told him stuff he didn't know about Big Eddy Colloch, who was not someone to mess with. Thinking, be extra careful, he said, "I ain't seen Eddy in a long time. My name's Larry, what's yours."

"I know who you are, Larry, but you don't need to know my name. We ain't goin' nowhere cause I'm here to deliver a message. But if it makes you feel better, you can call me Arlene."

"Okay, Arlene, but before you deliver your message, I've got to take a whiz." Larry didn't invite her to sit.

On his way to the restroom, Larry had thought of his deal with Poppy. *Something's going on here. Who the hell sent her after me? I better call Poppy and apologize for making such a stupid threat. Nonsense, my threats don't intimidate Poppy. I've threatened him before, and he ignores me. The worst thing about working with Poppy is he requires his people to check in with him more than I like checking in with anybody.* Then Larry remembered he had left the phone in his suit jacket folded on the booth seat.

He came out of the restroom and saw Billy blocking the narrow hallway glaring like an angry bull. "Goddammit, Larry. How many times do I have to tell you, stay away from my women? So, you bonk Roberta once in a while. That's okay, I don't care about that, but you better stay the hell away from Wesley."

"Who? What are you saying, Billy? Who's Wesley?"

Billy blinked. He blinked again. "You lying bastard. Wesley Chappelle! She's sitting in your fuckin' booth. Don't tell me you don't know her. I don't know why I put up with you, Larry."

Oh, Christ! Be careful now. There haven't been more than a handful of times I've seen Billy lose it, but somebody always regrets it. And it's never Billy. "I swear Billy, I never saw that woman until a few minutes ago. She told me her name is Arlene."

"It is Arlene," Billy growled. "Wesley Arlene Chappelle." He lunged. Larry stepped back and tripped as Billy rushed by. At the fire exit, Billy paused. He looked back at Larry and, in the soft voice that made those who respected his prowess refer to him as Whispering Bill, said, "I mean it, Larry. You keep pushing me, and you'll wish for the easy way out, like Big Eddy got. Even if you are my brother." Billy burst through the door and the alarm sounded. Larry fainted, hitting his head on the gumball machine.

Arlene heard the commotion and knew what was happening. Men fighting excited her, especially when the fight was about her. She found Larry sitting against the wall. "You take it easy, baby. Let me see if you're hurt."

"Hell yes, I'm hurt. Think I got a shiner."

Arlene's attitude startled Larry. She was suddenly all tender and caring that he may be injured. "Come on, let's get out of here and get some ice on that bump." She helped him to the Mustang. At her place, she cleaned his face and gave him a pain pill and a cold pack to hold to his eye. "I'll be back in a few minutes. You lie there and relax."

Larry realized his brother's threat had upset him, and he needed to relax and think about what to do next. He closed his eyes but couldn't make sense of what had happened. *Billy has been away for a few weeks because he flubbed a job, and Poppy got angry. Why is he back? Is Poppy okay with it? Does he know where Arlene lives? Maybe a nap will help me think.*

Arlene's kiss woke him. "The swelling is down, and I think your eye will be fine. She kissed him again. "It's time for me to find out if you are as good in the sack as I'm guessing. Then, I'm bettin' you're gonna need another nap."

A delicious aroma seeped into Larry's dream, and he awoke to see Arlene standing in the doorway smiling at him. His mouth watered, but he wasn't sure what was causing it, "What's that wonderful smell?"

"That, you beautiful man, is the aroma of a special recipe and my secret twist to cooking pork. It's almost ready."

Larry looked at his watch. *Crap, it's late. What the hell happened to the day? She cleaned my face. We had great sex, and I must have passed out. I don't know where I am, but I know I'm in trouble. Maybe Arlene or Wesley or whatever her real name is helping me, but maybe not. Why else would she have brought me here? But if she's for real, I can use her. She is a better sucker magnet than Roberta. She hooked Billy—turned him into a wild man. But she's hooked me too.*

Larry still lay sprawled on the bed when Arlene returned. "The pork's almost ready. But before we eat, I make the absolute best Hawaiian Slings you ever tasted in your life. Want one? Or two?"

Oh yeah, All I need is to get wasted when Poppy, Billy, and Jimmy are all pissed at me. "Sure."

Polishing off her second drink, Arlene said, "If you're ready, we can eat." Larry nodded and followed her to the table.

He took one bite and said, "Please tell the cook this is the best pork I ever ate and ask her to tell me her real name."

"Well, nobody calls her Wesley Arlene Chappelle, but her Daddy and close friends call her Wacko. She's always doing stuff they think is offbeat, like the tattoo of Little Eddy. Sounds silly, I know, but I think it fits. You like it?"

"Yeah, I do. But what I want to know, Wacko, is why did you bring me here? Why didn't you just drive away? You heard Billy."

"Oh, I heard him. And you should know, there's nothing between Billy and me. That's all in his mind."

"Does he know where you live?"

"Come on, Larry. He's never known. And another thing. Billy didn't do Big Eddy. It was Jimmy."

"Jimmy! Why?"

"He didn't like the way Eddy was treating me. He hinted big trouble was coming, and he saw no need for me to be involved. He told me not to waste effort trying to save Big Eddy because all the gears were grinding and the pieces falling."

"Okay, but why me?"

"Larry, Larry, Larry. You think you are the best-looking guy to come along since Robert Redford, and you're right. And your action in the sack, it's as good as or better than you think it is. And you know that has to be pretty damned good."

It had been a busy morning, and Larry was delighted that all Wacko's attributes were natural. The iguana had bothered him at first, but when he closed his eyes, it was as if the lizard wasn't there. "So, you got a plan?"

"I know you've been thinking about escaping from Poppy. I've found a place that's damn near paradise and with uninhabited islands. If we want to, we can go for weeks without seeing another person, then certainly not anybody we know."

Larry stared at Wacko. *She seems sincere, but it has to be a trap. But why the ruse? Why didn't they just take care of me? I violated the rules. Are they trying to torture me?* He said, "Tell me, Wacko, how did you learn about this paradise?"

"I was with a client from Switzerland. His houseboy liked me— a lot. One day he gave me some unbelievably good exotic dish. So, I did something unusually nice for him, and he told me about the place he was from."

"But how will we live," Larry asked.

"That's the easy part. It doesn't cost much to live there. We'll use the dough you get from Poppy."

Larry liked Wacko's plan, and he wanted her, but not the idea of having just one woman. "So, how long do we stay in this paradise? Forever?"

"We only need to stay until after the Revolution."

"What?"

"Yeah. Big changes are coming and you are gonna be a winner when it's over. Poppy and Billy are both in big trouble. That's the message I'm supposed to deliver."

"That's a lot to think about. What I don't get is why, with you and Jimmy being so close, I never heard of you?"

Wacko stood and walked into the kitchen. When she returned holding fresh drinks, she smiled and said, "I'm Jimmy's sister."

"Holy shit. Don't tell me that. Now I am in trouble."

"No, you're not. We don't interfere with each other, Jimmy and me. He calls me when he has a special job. And you are more special than you imagined. And I'm sure more than Jimmy imagines."

"This is a lot to take in. All a big surprise to me."

"I get that. If you want, you can leave and finish the trip I interrupted. Seventy-five Gs is a lot of money."

Standing close in front of him, she raised her arms over her head, stretching her abdomen taut. "But I think you are gonna want to stay with me and Little Eddy."

Wacko relaxed, and Little Eddy winked at Larry

.

I'm Leaving

That's it. I'm leaving. For good this time. I mean it. Goodbye.
I'm sorry.

So, what! I've known that for a long time—you rotten bastard.
You never change.

You know what I meant. I'm sorry you're leaving.

Do you mean because I'm finally leaving for good? I shoulda never
come back.

Please stay. I need you here.

You don't need me. You just want to have your way. You don't
need anybody. Not once have you ever shown any appreciation.
No matter how hard I try.

You know I'm no good at that kind of stuff.

I know you're no damned good. That's what I know.

Don't say that. Please. They'll hear you.

What do you care? If you cared at all, you would have changed the
first time I complained.

What am I gonna do without you? You're the best I've ever had.

Do you think that kind of talk helps?

What kind of talk?

The best you've ever had! Do you seriously think comparing me to your others makes me feel better? Makes me want to put up with more of your same ol' same ol'?

I really want you to stay. Nothing will be right without you.

You want! What about what I want? Do you ever give any thought to what I need? What I feel? What I think? You're selfish and insensitive, and I'm fed up with it. Goodbye.

No, wait! There has to be a way to fix this.

What way?

Look! You come rolling in here, and everything is fine, and suddenly you go thundering out. I just don't need that.

There, you admitted it. You don't need me.

You know I don't mean that. I do need you, and I'll change.

Ha! Fat chance.

I'll miss how you smell when you come through the door.

Smell? How do I smell?

You know. Allison Krauss says it in that song of hers, "Like moonlight and early morning rain."

Oh, God. Not again with the schmaltz. Why do you do this?

I don't know, but I blame you.

Yeah. I know. But it's you. You bastard. Give me one good reason not to haul ass for good.

Okay. The guys don't like that a woman can tune a Harley better than them, but it's true. You go, and I lose half my customers.

Damn it. You win. I'll stay, but you're going to give me a raise and buy me dinner.

And a bottle of wine.

Inspired by Alison Krauss and Union Station's *It Doesn't Have to Be This Way*

TRACKS IN THE SNOW

Walt sipped his second bourbon and settled into the recliner. He'd had a brisk walk with the dogs, who enjoyed being in the snow as much as Walt. Although the wind was stronger than he liked, walking in new snow invigorated his aging body. Last night, four inches of powder blanketed his mountain community. He was sorry Mary missed it, but she had chosen to visit with her college friends. Well, he had snow, bourbon, a fire, dogs, and his favorite school was in a major bowl game.

The front door burst open, and the wind blew swirls of snow into the entry hall. Sadie, the short-haired brown dog, was out the door and into the snow before Walt could get out of the recliner. Bozo got up to investigate and stood in the open doorway with snow eddying around him. When Walt reached for his collar, the dog bounded after Sadie.

In his slippers and sweats, the aging former athlete walked onto the porch and called to the dogs. They did not respond. He whistled his come-get-a-treat whistle, and Sadie stopped. She turned to look at him, then walked into the neighbor's yard and disappeared behind a hemlock. Bozo trotted behind her. The wind blew snow in Walt's face, and the cold, damp air made him shiver. He whistled again. The dogs did not come. A sudden roar of crowd noise called him back to the bowl game. He hesitated for a moment, but the game and the warmth of the fireplace beckoned. He shivered and went inside.

"Okay. Freeze your tails off. See if I care." Disgusted, Walt almost slammed the door.

Standing with his back to the fire, watching a replay of the Georgia touchdown, Walt thought about the dogs. He shrugged. *To hell with it. Bozo will follow Sadie and she'll come home.*

He settled into his recliner, sipped his bourbon and recalled his consternation when Mary adopted the dogs from the shelter where she volunteered. Before coming into the shelter, Sadie had run loose. Walt believed the dog was too old to train. She escaped at every opportunity, but she knew where to find food and a warm bed, so she always returned. Bozo was much younger and did not seem to get that he was supposed to come when called. Treats didn't help. Sometimes he came, and sometimes not. Still growing and shy, like an overprotected child, Bozo rarely had, even as a tiny puppy, been outside off his lead. He had given Walt no indication of being smart. Loving and sweet, but not smart. He would sit on command, but nothing else.

Walt drained the bourbon and went into the kitchen for another. From the kitchen window, through the trees against the snow-covered ground, he saw the dogs in his neighbor's backyard. He put his glass on the counter and walked out onto his deck to try once more to get them home. He whistled. Both dogs looked up. He called their names and whistled again. Sadie turned away, trotted down the hill, and disappeared into the trees. Bozo looked at Walt, then followed Sadie.

Back in the kitchen, he poured a fresh drink and returned to the game. At halftime, he changed the channel to check on the local weather. The weather girl gestured at a map covered with ominous symbols as she warned of more snow turning to freezing rain in his part of the North Georgia mountains.

Stupid sonsabitches! You'd think Sadie would know enough not to go out in this mess. He flipped back to the game and took a long pull of bourbon.

Walt tried, but he couldn't concentrate on the game. It was careless not to secure the door after walking the dogs. Although

Mary was fond of Sadie, he believed his wife had adopted the dog because no one else wanted her. The situation with Bozo was different. Mary loved him. She cuddled and talked to him like a little child. Walt pictured the disappointment on Mary's face when she learned that Bozo had been gone all night. *I can't let the little son-ofabitch stay out there. She'll kill me for letting him get away. He's too dumb to find his way home. What the hell? A little fresh air won't hurt.*

He put on boots and the red UGA parka Mary had given him on their first Christmas after retirement. He checked the pocket for dog treats and took his hiking stick from the closet and set off to find the dogs.

Walt liked being outdoors. He and Mary had chosen to retire in this sparsely populated community because of its easy access to mountain trails. From their deck, they could see out over the state forest adjoining the community. There were only a few summer cabins between their house and the forest, and they were empty and shuttered for the winter, which was okay with Walt; he and Mary enjoyed the solitude and the occasional snowstorms.

The dog tracks were easy to identify in the new snow. Walt knew Sadie, a hound mix, moved along straightforwardly with her nose close to the ground. Bozo, a mixed breed puppy, was another matter. Not yet a year old, he saw distractions everywhere, and this was his first experience at free play outside a fenced area. Mary refused to let him outside unless on a leash. Now he was out, loose and investigating fresh curiosities.

Walt walked downhill for ten more minutes before the tracks separated again. This divergence was different from the others. One set turned left, and the others turned right. He did not see them come together in the snowy woods ahead. Which one to follow? Did it matter? He knelt in the snow and tried to see a difference in the tracks. There should be a depression where the shorter Sadie's low-slung chest may have scarred the snow between her footmarks, but he saw nothing to help.

He told himself the dogs would stay together. But the way the tracks parted made him believe otherwise. He looked at the woods and the snow-covered hill sloping away before him. The undergrowth and flecks of falling snow made him uncertain of what was beyond a small opening ahead. Walt liked to tell people he was a hiker, but he knew he was just a trail walker who didn't understand orienteering, never bothered learning survival techniques and did not know how to track. He took a few steps and knelt again, trying to discern a difference between the two sets of tracks. The snow began to change to large, heavy flakes.

Damn snow. It'll cover the tracks, and I won't be able to follow either set. He thought about the warm fire and repressed the desire for a drink. From his coat pockets, he took gloves and a skullcap. He reminded himself it would take him twice as long to go back uphill, and Mary's of disappointment.

No dammit! I've let her down too many times. She deserves better. I've got to look a little longer. Walt whistled, called the dogs by name, and whistled again. He always whistled at feeding and treat times. He waited and scanned for movement, hoping at least one dog would answer the whistle. Nothing. He whistled again and marveled at how quiet the woods are in the snow.

For no specific reason, he chose the left leading tracks and had moved only a few steps down the slope when his foot slid. He jammed the hiking stick into the snow, but it slipped on the icy rock beneath. He shifted his weight and reached for a sapling to steady himself, but he missed it. He was sliding down the hill.

Whoa, dummy! Oh God, I forgot the rock ledge.

His left knee buckled, and his weight landed on his bent leg when he fell. Pain knifed through his knee as he fell onto his back and slid downhill headfirst, thinking about the drop-off somewhere in front of him. He managed to roll over enough to see the rock right before his head hit it.

He awoke on his side with his chest against an oak tree. *God Almighty, what happened? How long have I been here?* Struggling to clear his mind, he tried to move, but intense pain in his knee stopped him. Tingling fingers made him realize his left arm was trapped under his body. A little more movement worked his arm free. Massaging his hands, he felt his fingers coming back to life. He placed both hands against the tree and pushed away from the trunk. "Aaiieee! Oh God that hurts." He gasped for air, inhaling deeper with each breath until the pain in his knee subsided. *Damned knee. I should've had it fixed when Doc told me to. What did I do to my head? It's killing me.*

He removed a glove and wiped tears from his face. The crimson smear on his hand startled him. He looked down at the red stain where his head had touched the snow while he was unconscious. Above his temple, the sticky, drying blood covered a large, tender lump. He checked his fingertips and wiped them in the snow to remove the blood. He touched the wetness again. The cut was not significant, and the snow had staunched the blood flow. He held a loose ball of snow to his head, hoping it would ease the pain.

The snow felt good against his aching head, but the cold made his hand hurt. He looked at the snowball, decided the bleeding was not enough to worry about, and tossed it away. He put his glove on and carefully tried to shift his weight without moving the throbbing knee. He felt and poked it as he had seen his doctors do. *I know it's a mess. Always has been, but I don't know what else is wrong.* His ankle was tender, but the knee was the problem. It hurt all the time, and the pain intensified when he moved it. He thought through his options and laughed when he found himself trying to decide if it had been good luck that the tree kept him from sliding off the ledge. *If I'm unable to walk, I'll probably freeze to death. It might be better to have gone over.*

He thought of calling for help, but his phone was by the recliner. He remembered there was no signal where he sat. Before his pneumonia last summer, he hiked here often and knew the phone would be useless. He decided not to waste his energy yelling for help. His neighbors were away and all the houses down the hill were empty for the winter. The only year-round people were uphill on the other side of the crest, and his voice would not carry that far, even on a clear day.

It took him a long time to maneuver so he could use the tree as a backrest. He leaned back and closed his eyes to let the pain ease. After a few minutes, he worked his pants leg up over his knee. The swelling looked familiar. He had seen it before—once in high school and again as a college sophomore when his football career ended on a linebacker's helmet. He packed snow on it.

Once beyond the shock of the cold against his bare skin, the cold eased the pain. Exertion and bourbon worked on his injured sixty-eight-year-old body. It felt good to relax. *I'm just gonna sit here and rest. Then I'm going home. Damn dogs. To hell with 'em. I wish I had an aspirin. My head hurts bad.*

He closed his eyes, and the snow continued.

"What the?" A tongue licking his face startled Walt. Bozo nuzzled closer. "Why didn't you show up when I called you? Stupid mutt. Where's your sister?"

Walt looked around but saw no sign of the other dog. He took a dog biscuit from his coat pocket, whistled, and gave Bozo the treat. The dog ate it and lay down beside Walt. Despite pretended annoyances and frequent protests to Mary, Walt was fond of Bozo. He was too big to be a lap dog, but otherwise, he was perfect for the role. Once he understood it was okay to get onto your lap, he contentedly lay motionless until told to move.

He gave Bozo another biscuit and took off a glove and stroked the dog's fur, massaging his neck and behind his ears while Bozo snuggled against his master's outstretched leg. "You don't look too bad. Some ice balled between your toes and on the long hairs of your belly and tail. You like this weather, Bozo?"

As Walt worked ice from between the dog's toes, he was once more amazed at how Bozo accepted grooming. The dog offered no resistance and seemed never to tire of the attention. "I may as well admit I like you, Bozo. But don't tell Mary."

Walt pulled his hood over his head and relaxed against the tree. With his gloved hands in his pockets and the dog's warm body against his leg, he drifted off again. While he slept, the large soft flakes grew heavier, slowly morphing into light, freezing rain.

The cold caused the sleeping man to move his exposed leg, and sharp pain in his knee awakened him. *Dammit! You know better than to go into the woods when you've been drinking.* He placed a small clump of snow in his mouth to ease the cottony dryness of sleep. His head ached. *I wish I had an aspirin.*

Bozo stood and moved a few steps away, leaving a warm place against Walt's good leg. *You're a good heater, Bozo. You should have been next to my bare leg.* The dog watched the man push the packed snow away from his knee and rub the bare skin to warm it before pulling his pant leg down.

Walt considered Bozo's wet brown eyes. "I must've whacked my head pretty hard on that rock. I think I passed out. It's getting dark." He squinted and moved his watch back and forth, trying to focus. *Good God! It's late, and I gotta get home. I'm cold.*

Using the tree for support, he pulled himself upright and eased more weight onto his left leg. "Okay, let's see how this knee's gonna work. Now is not the time to wimp out. I gotta get home before dark."

For the first time, Walt looked uphill toward home. He could see nothing other than the dark lines of trees against the snow. A low-lying dark cloud hid the top of the mountain. "Oh crap. I'm in trouble. See what you got me into, dog." His heart skipped. *Stop it man. You don't have heart trouble. You may be frightened, but you have a strong heart. Now suck it up and get home. Where is that damned hiking pole?*

Fresh snow had almost covered the scar from his slide, but Walt could see the stick a few feet away. He braced one hand on the tree and slid his right foot toward the target and pushed off from the tree. He knew the fall was coming and put his hands out and eased his body to the snow.

He reached for the stick. "Come on, just a little more. Bozo, why did Mary choose you and not a retriever." Grasping the stick, he struggled upright.

"Okay, now what? Do we go up or down? You don't have a clue, do you boy?" The dog cocked his head to one side.

Walt was afraid to go straight uphill and risk sliding back down the icy rock. He considered going down to the only road between himself and the state forest, but all the houses in between were summer houses. *Down to a road with little or no traffic or a shorter steep climb home.* He knew his knee would hurt more going down-hill than up. He also knew it would be much less strenuous to walk downhill. In July, he had caught a cold that turned into pneumo-nia. He had not yet gotten his stamina back and wanted to avoid the climb. Down was appealing.

"Hey Bozo, I just remembered the stream. That knock on the head must have addled my brain. Where is it? I haven't crossed it yet." Walt cupped his hands around his eyes to concentrate his vi-sion in the poor light. He thought he could see a thin dark line through the trees where a rill carried water from a small spring to the lake in the valley below. *That settles it. I'm barely a third of the way down.* "We're going up the hill. C'mon Bozo."

Moving along the contour line to get around the slippery rock made his left foot lower, adding pressure on his injured knee, and with each step it hurt more. Beyond the outcropping, Walt started uphill. Going up hurt less than moving across the slope, and the hiking pole helped. After a few yards, he stopped to get his breath. He was tired, and it took too long for his breathing to return to normal. His knee throbbed all the time, and there were frequent sharp jolts of pain.

The freezing rain continued.

Petting Bozo's head and giving him another biscuit, he said, "Let's go, dog. I didn't come out in this mess just to leave you here." He took a few more steps uphill. His foot slipped, and he fell on his face. The dog sniffed at Walt's face. Walt cursed and struggled to his feet. "Bozo, I'm glad you don't understand that I have injured my dignity."

A few more steps and he was breathing hard again. *I can't tell if I'm making progress or the cloud's getting lower. Damn, it's cold.* His steps no longer made a crunch sound. Now there was a crack, then a crunch, but Walt didn't notice.

Bozo moved around Walt as though shepherding him. *I'm not sure if I'm going toward the house. Too far to the left, and I miss the road. Then I'm in deep trouble. I gotta get home before dark.* Peering up the hill, he could see barely fifty yards through the dim light, and nothing looked familiar.

"C'mere Bozo. Come on, boy." The dog bounded to the man and licked his face as Walt bent down to pet him. "Go home, Bozo. Go home, boy. Go home, find Mary." The dog looked up, cocked his head to one side. "Go home! Find Mary. Find Mary." Walt played this game with Bozo every day when he took him for walks. When they were a hundred or so yards from home, he liked to let Bozo off leash and tell him to go home and find Mary. Sometimes the dog turned and ran full speed to their front door. Other times, he just stared as though he had no idea what Walt expected.

"Come on, boy, I need you to show me the way home. Every step is like hell, and I can't see the house. Go home, Bozo! Find Mary!" The dog turned and bolted up the steep hill. After a few yards, he veered to his left and ran toward what Walt hoped was home. Once more, he started moving up the mountain, squinting into the fading light.

His head throbbed and his knee and ankle hurt terribly. With each step, needle-sharp pain exploded in his knee. His back ached from limping. *God, my legs are cold.* He bent down and rubbed his legs, trying to warm them. He realized his pants legs were wet. He looked at the ice on his sleeves and gloves and shook his head. *Thank God Mary gave me a waterproof coat.*

Walt laughed aloud, recalling his wife's laughter when he opened the box Christmas morning. "Don't look so startled, Dear. It'll keep you dry and warm when we hike. I thought you would like a coat in UGA red. Though I still don't understand how any-one from Vermont can be such a rabid Georgia football fan."

Mary was right. Under the coat I am dry and warm. Every other part of me is wet and cold.

He rested against a tree, rubbing the backs of his hands to-gether, knocking the ice off his gloves. *How could I have been stupid enough to get into this situation?* He tried to see his watch. "Dammit, Walt. What's happened to your brains? You bought a watch you can't read without your glasses?" He moved the watch back and forth, trying to focus. A sinking feeling hit his belly when he real-ized he had been out more than three hours. "It'll be dark soon. Come on, get to it."

He dragged his tired, hurting body another ten yards up the hill. With each step, the ice layer over the snow seemed to be harder to break. He fell again, and the hiking stick slipped from his grasp. He gave silent thanks for the wrist loop and told himself he couldn't make it without the pole. *I may not make it anyway.*

He pulled himself upright. *Don't think like that. You have to make it. Take one step at a time. You gotta have the damn knee fixed anyway. Stop worrying about the pain. Just get up the hill. Come on. Do it, dammit.* He jammed the pole into the snow and stepped for-ward with his right leg, then dragged his left leg to the pole. Again.

Again. He stopped and took a deep breath. The wet, freezing air hurt his lungs.

He thought he heard a dog barking. Walt looked uphill. *Damned cloud. How can they be so pretty from a distance and so nasty when you're in them?* He stepped forward once more. The leg hurt all over and felt like a useless load as he dragged it up the hill. *Christ, this is one steep hill. Why the hell did I ever move to this god-awful mountain?*

Step. Pull. Step. Pull. "Remember to breathe. What are you? Stupid? Breathe."

Step. His foot didn't go through the ice.

Stomp. Stomp.

He tried to step forward but slipped. Facedown in the icy snow, he struggled, gasping, trying to make his breathing regular. When it settled, he wondered if Bozo was home. *My beautiful Mary. I hope you're having a wonderful time. It feels good to be off my feet. Oh God, I'm tired. I'm gonna lie here and rest a minute, then start again.*

He heard a dog bark.

Which one is that?

It doesn't matter. I have to rest.

SOMETHING RED

For five years, Mary and her college friends have met every January at Callaway Gardens. It is a beautiful place, and she has a better time with her friends now than when they were young. But for the first time since the group started their reunions, thoughts of leaving early have nagged her since dinner. Snuggled under the covers, she is missing Walt. *Georgia won, and I'm sorry I wasn't there for his delightful antics when his team won. He must have enjoyed the early snowfall and the ballgame—and his bourbon.*

The storm had moved farther south than predicted and hit the higher elevations in the North Georgia mountains. She knew their house would have several inches of snow, she hoped the ice missed their community, but from experience, she knew better.

She wishes she had skipped the reunion with her friends. Callaway Gardens is lovely but walking in the snow with Walt and the dogs is so much fun.

Mary cares nothing for college football, but Walt is a fan. After all their years together, she still enjoys having him point out subtleties in the game. She thinks of the dogs lying between Walt and the hearth, missing her home and husband and their snowy mountain. *I'll leave after breakfast, and the girls will have to accept it.*

Mary says goodbye despite her friends' protests. She telephones, but Walt doesn't answer—*he must be walking the dogs.* She leaves a message that she will be home for a late lunch with him— confident the road crews will have plowed and sanded by then.

A few miles from home, she sees the first snow accumulations. On the drive up the mountain road leading her house, ice-coated trees sparkle in the late morning sun, adding extra life to the brilliant, ever-changing winter landscape she and her husband find so delightful. She hopes Walt has cleared their driveway. He has asked her not to drive on it because the car's weight packs the snow and ice and makes it harder for him to clear it.

Mary stops at the driveway entrance and sees her dog, Sadie, run into the front yard. She reaches for her boots in the back of the Jeep while Sadie whines and barks beside the car.

She holds on to trees and shrubs for support to make her way across the yard to the front door making, chirping happy noises to Sadie, who slips on the ice as she runs around Mary. *She's barking more than usual. Walt must have let you out because of the weather, and I don't blame him for not going out again.*

She opens the door and calls his name, but there is no answer.

She calls again. No answer. *He must be in the bathroom.*

Sadie sits at her feet, whining. At the coat closet, Mary hangs her coat and trades her boots for house shoes. Walt's red UGA parka is not on the hanger. *I guess he and Bozo don't move as fast in this weather as Sadie does.*

She sees Walt's bourbon glass and a snack plate by Walt's recliner in the great room—the bourbon watery from melted ice and sandwich half-eaten. *Just like him. Had as much as he wanted and left the rest. Didn't expect me until tonight and went to bed without picking up. He knows I hate that, but he does it anyway. He must not have checked the answering machine.* She picks up the dishes and takes them to the kitchen. The bourbon bottle and sandwich makings sit on the counter.

That man. A seventy-year-old little boy. Forty-five years I've been trying, and he won't change. Still preoccupied, she doesn't notice there are no coffee cups or other dishes.

"Bozo. Come, Bozo." Mary calls her puppy, disappointed he didn't greet her as she came into the house. Sadie continues getting underfoot, and Mary, assuming the dog is glad to see her, bends down to pet her, but the dog whines and runs barking to the back door.

"You just came in, lady. I'm not going to let you out so soon." She walks to the bedroom, calling Walt. There is no answer, but Sadie keeps barking.

She is surprised to see the bed made. *There is just no way to predict what that man will do. He makes the bed but won't put away his dirty dishes.* She shouts, "Walt. I'm home!" Silence.

Sadie whines again. "I said no, Sadie. You just came inside." Mary notices the master bath is dark. *Where can that man be?* As Mary walks toward the basement stairs, Sadie whines louder. "Just a minute Sadie. I want to find Walt and Bozo."

She peers down the stairs. The lights are not on. "Walt! Are you down there?" No answer.

Shoot, his hearing is so bad he won't know I'm up here. Mary starts down the steps but pauses, a sudden empty feeling in her stomach. *Bozo never goes down the stairs. They have to be outside.* A vision of the coat closet pops into her head. Walt's red coat. *That's it. But why is Sadie by herself?*

Mary rechecks the closet. Finally irritated at Sadie's noise and agitation, she says, "Okay. Okay. I'll let you out." At the word out, the dog runs to the back door and barks again.

Despite Sadie's noise and pawing at the door, Mary manages to open it. Sadie runs across the icy deck, losing her footing when she turns to go down the steps. Her legs never stop moving as she scrambles upright and almost slides down the icy steps.

Something is wrong. Sadie only barks at bears and possum, and they won't be out today. Mary inches her way across the slippery deck and looks down at Sadie barking and trying to run on the icy, snow-covered yard.

"What's wrong, Sadie? Where's Walt?"

At the mention of Walt's name, Sadie scrambles through the trees to a lower corner of the steep backyard, barking the entire time. She stops and looks back at Mary. Mary cups her hands around her eyes and strains to see through the dark tree trunks.

Sadie walks farther into the wooded yard and paws at something. It moves, and Mary thinks she sees Bozo raise his head, and she squints harder.

"Bozo? Yes, it is Bozo. Bozo! Come, boy."

Bozo barks and Mary calls again, "Come on, Bozo. Come."

Whining and barking, Sadie paws at Bozo. He struggles to stand. His dark, thick fur is icy. He shakes himself and takes a step, then raises his head and howls, startling Mary. She has never heard either dog howl.

Bozo turns back to where he had been lying, and both dogs paw at something red.

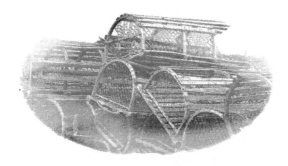

EPHRAIM'S LOBSTER POT

My hometown has its share of harmless eccentrics. Mother's older brother was one of those people. Ephraim's antics always drew laughter that he seemed not to understand, although on rare occasions, after a long pause, he would break into an infectious giggle. He was well-liked in town, and folks enjoyed his good-natured approach to life.

He was a small man who did not attract attention when he dressed in ordinary clothing. The townspeople were accustomed to seeing Ephraim appear in foul weather gear on a sunny July day. But no one could ignore him on that extra warm day he appeared on the village green dressed in a yellow slicker and pulling a little red wagon. With an unsmiling face, he introduced summer visitors to Clark, his pet watermelon. The next day, Clark Melon shared the wagon with his sister Millie Melon. I suspect that even today, after all this time, a mention of Ephraim's name at Womble's Bar still makes the regulars share hearty laughter and tales of summer visitors reacting to Ephraim and his pet watermelons.

Dad and Ephraim were good friends and co-owned a lobster boat. Ephraim was a good-natured worker who did not waste time talking. Dad appreciated Ephraim's reticence and energetic work and ignored most of the peculiarities. But occasionally, Ephraim said or did something that, although comical, caused Dad to worry and express concern about whether Ephraim did those silly things because he was single and lived alone and was bored, or genuinely had a screw loose.

Dad had a reason for his concern, but he did not share it with me until high school. Mom had been pregnant with me when her mother showed signs of dementia. Her health deteriorated rapidly, and she died in the asylum at Augusta before I was three. After Grandma's funeral, Dad and Mom learned that her grandmother had suffered a similar fate. Naturally, he was worried about Mom and Ephraim. Although he had not shared that information until he believed I was old enough to understand, I had known he was concerned since my twelfth birthday.

The day before my birthday, Dad took me with him to pick up something he needed from a town down the coast. When we returned, Thelma Womble approached Dad while I was still in the boat cabin, and she didn't know I was there.

Thelma said, "Afternoon, Nate."

"Afternoon, Thelma. I've not seen you down here lately."

"Need to talk, and I figured this is a good place to catch you."

"What's going on?"

"Sara was in the store this morning. Bought a birthday present."

"That's good. We've been talking about what to get Silas. Hard to believe the boy's already twelve."

"Well, it's not good, Nate. She bought a dress for her daughter."

Dad fell back as though she had slapped him. His thin body slumped against the boat. His head drooped, and neither of them said anything for a while. At last, he mumbled what sounded like, "Thank you for letting me know, Thelma."

She said, "I'm sorry, Nate. But I thought you should know before you got home."

He did not look up until Thelma's footsteps faded, then I heard him say softly, "She's only thirty-nine."

Maybe it was because Dad looked so stricken, but I kept quiet and did not ask him why Mom would buy a present for a daughter she did not have. He did not mention Thelma's visit to the boat. Ephraim came to dinner the next night, and we celebrated my birthday without any mention of what Thelma told Dad.

I loved Uncle Ephraim, and after all these years, thinking of him still makes me smile. When I was five or six, I told Mother that Uncle Eph's eyes twinkled, and he made me laugh. His eyes really did twinkle, especially so when he laughed with his stubby little tobacco pipe clenched in his teeth. His laughter was soft, high-pitched and giggly. People near enough to hear him found the sound amusing, and they laughed with him.

When Mom's spells, as she and Dad called them, came, they passed quickly, though occasionally one lasted several hours. Despite her memory loss, Dad had to work the boat. One night, after Mom was in bed, he told me that after my grandmother died, he, Mom and Ephraim had talked with Thelma Womble and other old-timers, and that's when they learned my great-grandmother had also had periods of not knowing what was real. No one recalled any men in the family having problems—except Ephraim.

Dad was stoic in dealing with the situation. I was old enough to care for myself and be aware when Mom had problems, but he worried about her when I was at school. I did my best to follow Dad's lead in dealing with Mom's illness, but, honestly, it was not an easy thing for me to do.

Mom's mind wandered increasingly, and her spells came more often and lasted longer. By my fourteenth birthday, she could not recognize any of her family or care for herself. I know it broke Dad's heart to do it, but he yielded to her doctor's advice that she would be less danger to herself in the state hospital. He was never talkative, but he was unusually quiet the day we drove Mom to the hospital. On the way home, he suddenly said, "Silas, have you noticed that Eph's nutty behavior has stopped?"

"No, sir. I've been so concerned about Mom I haven't thought anything about Ephraim. "

"Well, as far as I know, he hasn't pulled any of his stunts since Sara started having problems."

After that, when school was not in session, I went with him and Ephraim to work in the boat. I tried to help, but there was so much I did not know. Although I had no interest in learning, Ephraim was exceptionally kind and welcomed me aboard. He was patient as he taught me about their work. There are times when I wish I had liked lobstering, but I came close to hating it.

Once or twice a week, Ephraim came to our house for dinner, and at least once a week, we all ate at Womble's Bar. We were there the night Ephraim told Dad he would no longer work the lobster traps on Wednesdays.

"I'm sorry, Nate. I'll do everything else on Wednesdays, but life will be a lot better if I stay ashore on that day."

Dad tried to get an explanation, but Ephraim evaded answering until, at last, he looked straight at his brother-in-law and said, "To tell the truth, Nate, I'm afraid I'll catch a mermaid."

Well, that struck both of us silent. The only alternative was to laugh, thinking it was just another of Eph's nutty acts.

As Dad and I walked home, we both admitted to worrying that Ephraim might be succumbing to the illness that had killed his mother and grandmother.

A few weeks after Eph's announcement, Thelma Womble told us she had seen Ephraim in Freeport walking close and cozy with a young woman. "You should have seen her. She's such a tiny little thing, so short she makes Ephraim look tall. A great mass of light reddish-golden hair and fair features. She really stood out from the crowd in her sea-green dress and that hair. She was beautiful— much too pretty for the likes of Ephraim."

Ephraim with a woman was news. He had never shown any interest in women. When Dad asked him about the woman in Freeport, Ephraim blushed.

"She's a widow, Nate. She was married to Hank Perceval. He was a waterman up by Freeport. Storm caught him about four years back. Her name's Wednesday."

"Is that why you quit pulling pots on Wednesday? Because that's her name?"

Ephraim looked down as though he were embarrassed. He shifted his pipe to the other side of his mouth, then looked up, grinning around the pipe clamped between his teeth, "Well, to her, Wednesday is a special day. She asked me not to, and I said okay."

"She has you hooked. Right, Eph."

"C'mon, Nate. We got work to do."

By the time he announced he and Wednesday were getting married, Ephraim's only noticeable peculiarity was his unwavering refusal to work the pots on Wednesday.

When people asked Dad about it, he answered "Dunno" or "Not sure." He did not mention catching a mermaid.

I loved my new Aunt Wednesday, especially when I realized she was treating me as an adult. Sunday family dinners at Ephraim and Wednesday's house became the high point of my life.

Dad had difficulty keeping a helper willing to work only on Wednesdays. Some found full-time jobs and quit. He fired others because they were too slow, too cautious, or too talkative.

One day he said, "Eph's buying himself a boat. When school's out in June, I need you to help me. Don't plan on goin' back. Ten years is enough school for a waterman."

I didn't object. Although I had no interest in lobstering, school bored me, and I wanted to help Dad. Aunt Wednesday's presence had made Mother's death easier to bear, but I still missed her terribly. Working on the boat would keep me close to Dad. I soon became a competent lobsterman, and my work satisfied Dad. Life was good until my Selective Service draft notice arrived.

The notice disappointed me, but I was not reluctant to go into the Army. During those two years, I missed my family, especially during my time in Korea. I must have learned it from Dad, but I do not dwell on things beyond my control. I wrote long letters home and looked forward to Dad's reports about Eph and Wednesday and work. Honestly, I even enjoyed Dad's weather reports.

I was nearing the end of my service when Dad wrote, "Do you think you want to work the boat when you get home? If not, I may sell it and work at something else." He added a P.S., "Wednesday is sick, but Eph says you shouldn't worry. It's only a bad cold."

But the following letter brought horrible news: "Son, I am sorry to tell you Wednesday is dead. Her cold turned into pneumonia. They put her in the hospital, but she didn't make it. Eph is taking it hard. Have you thought about the boat?"

As soon as possible, I hurried home, but Dad's letters had not prepared me for the change in Ephraim. Those once twinkly eyes were dull and rheumy. There was no laughter. Even during private visits, his responses to questions were short, often no more than ah-yuh or naw. Sometimes he did not bother to answer. Although Ephraim had returned to work after a mourning period, he spoke only enough to transact business. He stopped leaving his house other than to work or to buy groceries. Before Wednesday's illness, she had kept their house spotless, but by the time I got back home, it looked as though no one had cleaned it since her death. I offered to help or even clean it myself.

Ephraim rejected the offers, and I felt I was intruding.

The war in Korea changed me more than I had realized. I was restless and no longer enjoyed evenings at Womble's. My old friends had married or moved away. Regular customers told me the place did not feel the same since light-hearted old Eph stopped coming in. Dad and I tried to help him out of his depression, but nothing we did helped. Some days we sat on the pier and watched the once jaunty man trudge uphill toward his empty house. I had been home for months and had not seen my uncle smile.

Finally, I decided to find a job and move to Brunswick. As much as I loved Dad and enjoyed being around him, Ephraim's sadness dragged down both of our spirits. Before I mustered the will to tell Dad my plan to move, he suffered a fatal heart attack.

His death made me unwilling to put up with my uncle's silence. At Ephraim's house, we would sit and stare down the hill, beyond the wharf to the water. Though I still loved the view, it did nothing to relieve my boredom or the restlessness that was building. For two consecutive visits, Ephraim's only response had been to nod and shift his pipe to the other side of his mouth, and I got angry.

A waterman from a town down coast bought Dad's boat, and I found work in Brunswick. I was surprised at how easy it was to leave the rented house where I was born and move away.

In early autumn 1954, I remembered Ephraim's 60th birthday was approaching, and I wanted to see my uncle. He had brought so much laughter into my young life, and it was time to put my anger aside and visit him. Realizing that Ephraim's birthday fell on Wednesday made me laugh out loud. Ephraim would not be on the water, making it a good day to pay him at least one more visit and wish him a happy birthday.

While I waited for Ephraim to answer the door, I noticed his house had been freshly painted. No one answered the door, so I opened it. As far as I know, Eph has never locked it. The house sparkled with cleanliness and order, but no one was there or in the work shed behind the house.

Rather than wait, I walked to Womble's Bar, the best place to find out what was going on. The village and the bar were more crowded than I recalled them being that time of year. John Womble, the fourth member of his family to own and run the place, shouted from behind the bar. "Good to see you, Silas. So, you heard about it in Brunswick, did you? Take a seat. Have a beer. On the house. Been far too long."

"Heard what, John? I came to wish Ephraim a happy birthday, but he's not home. What's going on?"

"Two things. Some folks are all excited because they heard Norman Rockwell is hanging around."

"The *Saturday Evening Post* guy? What's he doing here?"

"Some people say he's scouting subjects for a magazine cover. Ain't had so much excitement since Judge Foster's wife caught him with Peggy Morgan. But your uncle is the one who got my attention this morning."

"That's why I'm here. Is Eph okay?"

"Well, I don't know if he's okay. But he went out in his boat this morning with his pots. The last time he went out on a Wednesday, Pop still ran this place, and that seems like ages ago."

"What? He's pulling pots on Wednesday?"

"I'm surprised as you are. He let the gear and his house go to ruin. Some of his traps got in such bad shape there's no way they'd hold a big lobster. I'm surprised his boat stayed afloat."

"I stopped at his house. It looked great."

John held his hand up and moved to serve beers to customers at the other end of the bar. When he returned, he leaned toward me and grinned. "Don't know why, but three or four months back, old Ephraim, started sprucing things up. Some think he might finally be over grieving. He re-roofed and painted the house. He repaired his boat and his gear, so it looks first-rate. He's even been in here a few times. This morning topped it all."

John had more customers to tend, so I nursed my beer, kept an eye on the path to Eph's house, and listened to the customers speculate why Norman Rockwell was nosing around. About mid-afternoon, I saw a familiar-looking man lugging a bulky load. He seemed to be about Ephraim's height, but that load looked heavy, and his step had too much bounce to be my sad old uncle. But I wasn't sure, so I left my beer and went to find out who could be hauling such a load toward Ephraim's house.

I passed another man standing to one side and working on a sketch pad. When I caught up, it was Ephraim carrying a lobster trap on his back. A really big fish tail stuck out of the trap's low end, but the fish was not the usual color. From its head to the dorsal fin, it was the bright golden-red of a red snapper.

"Ephraim!"

Ephraim turned. With his little unlit pipe clamped between his teeth, he said, "Afternoon, Silas. Good of you to stop by. Been ages. How are you, nephew?" Ephraim's eyes sparkled just as they had before Wednesday died.

I could see Eph's muscles straining and offered to help, but Ephraim laughed and did not slow his pace, "I been waitin' a long time to carry this load. I'll manage it. Thanks all the same."

"Why, after all this time, did you go back to working traps on Wednesday?" His talkative response surprised me.

"When I met my beautiful Wednesday, she asked me not to pull pots on her namesake day. Cockamamie ideas about me catchin' and runnin' off with a mermaid on her special day. I always felt bad about Nate havin' to work around my promise." He paused to shift the load higher on his back. "Me catchin' a mermaid. Humph. Till she got sick, 'twas our private joke." Ephraim paused and looked toward his home.

"A terrible time, Silas. So bad sick and feverish." He resumed walking at his jaunty pace until he reached his house. He stared for a long moment at the door, then turned back to me. "She told me if I'd keep my promise till my 60th birthday, she'd come back to me if I could catch her again." He grinned and shook his head.

"When I realized my birthday fell on Wednesday, I figured she meant for me to pull my pots today."

Ephraim looked straight at me and nodded at the load on his back, and said, "I'm glad you came to visit, but I have to get this into the holding tank in my work shed. I'm tellin' my favorite nephew g'bye now." He turned and walked away.

On my way to my car, I saw the tall, unusually thin man who had been observing Ephraim climbing the hill. He had gray hair and looked to be about Ephraim's age but was much too well-dressed and distinguished-looking to be a lobsterman. Like Ephraim, he worked with his pipe clamped between his teeth, and he was concentrating on his sketchpad.

As I approached, he stopped drawing and looked up. He smiled and removed his pipe. He said, "Interesting-looking fellow, that waterman. Do you know him well?"

"He's my uncle."

"Do you think he'll agree to pose for a painting?"

I tried to be polite, but the question shocked me. "You'll have to ask Ephraim."

On the drive back to Brunswick, I felt good knowing that Ephraim was happy and cheerful again. He had seemed glad to see me, and I resolved to make a more extended visit.

Not long after talking with Eph, I found a better job. The new work was enjoyable, but it was exhausting. For a long time, work and spending time with my girlfriend kept me busy, and thoughts about Eph popped up only occasionally. Then, one day in late August, I picked up a copy of the new *Saturday Evening Post*. I thought Ephraim was on the cover—the same cap, boots, and pipe. The posture and the lobster pot on his back, even the apron, made me see Ephraim. His face was different, but the expression looked like his. And the mermaid in the lobster pot had hair the same color as Aunt Wednesday's.

SHE USED TO

Yes. That's my name.

- - -

What did you say?

- - -

A detective? Is that policeman with you?

- - -

What did you say? You must speak louder.

- - -

How am I? I'm lonesome. That's how I am.

- - -

My wife? No. She used to be here, but not anymore.

- - -

Well, I don't know where she is. She must be lost because she is not here.

- - -

I don't understand why you want to talk to me but come inside. I'm lonesome and it'll be nice to have company.

- - -

What say?

- - -

Yes. I'm sure my wife isn't home. That's why I'm lonesome. What do you want to talk about?

- - -

Eh? Could you please speak more clearly?

- - -

No, I don't remember when she left. I'm by myself and lonesome.

- - -

No, I don't know where she is. She didn't tell me goodbye. She must have gone somewhere because she isn't here. At least, I can't find her, and I've looked all over my part of the house. We can sit at the kitchen table. It will be okay if we do not touch the food. That would make her angry.

- - -

Do you like that platter? It is twelve inches by nine inches. Or is it vice-versa? I'm not sure which—and she's not here to tell me. I used to know, and if I couldn't remember, she used to tell me if I asked. Sometimes even if I didn't ask, she used to say, sweetheart, are you confused? Isn't that a great term? Used to. What in hell does used to mean?

- - -

What say?

- - -

No, I didn't call the police. If she wanted to go away that's her business even if I'm by myself and lonesome.

- - -

What's that?

- - -

Yes, I have hearing aids, but I don't know where they are either. They're lost just like she is. When she was here, I knew. And I cared. At least I thought I did. What in hell does cared mean, anyway? The broccoli on the platter is green and the meat is brown because it is cooked as it is supposed to be, and not raw and pink as it should not be when it's served to a human being.

- - -

Did I cook it? No. She cooked it. I don't know how to cook. When she lived here, she used to cook. Things were different, and I shaved. Do you like my beard? It used to be forty paces from the front door to the end of the driveway where the woman who delivers the morning paper in her car throws it. Now, I'm not sure how far it is. Sometimes it's too far and sometimes not far enough.

Now the dog isn't here either. He died. He used to retrieve the paper every morning. Isn't that a great term? Used to. I just love it. There are thirteen steps to, or from, the basement. She used to tell me we don't need a basement. But I said where else will we keep all the stuff we don't want to keep up here where we live?

- - -

Yes, she cooked this dinner.

- - -

What?

- - -

No, I never eat dinner unless she's at the table. I hold her chair so she can sit down first.

- - -

No, she didn't tell me she was leaving. I came in to eat dinner, and she wasn't waiting for me to hold her chair. She didn't tell me, and I don't know where she went. I used to get up at 5:30. Now I may, or I may not. I never know which it will be. It's a game I sometimes play with myself. Ha. Play with myself. That's a joke. Get it? Anyway, she's gone now. I miss her and that's a treat because when she used to live here, I thought she was a bother. I'm not bothered anymore, but I am lonesome.

- - -

What do I do? I wake up and I get up and take my goddamn pills. So many pills she used to put them in a little box with compartments to keep them in sequence—you know, in order, so I will know what to take when. But now they are not. I've always liked vice-versa. It sounds so much more official than on the other hand. And that's what I am—official—sitting at the head of the table talking to you gentlemen. You are official, at least you act official, and you told me you are, and he is wearing a uniform.

- - -

When I was her husband, I knew what I was, and now I don't know whether I am or not. She's gone, and I'm not sure what I am anymore, and nothing makes any difference. She's not here. At least she's not where I can find her. I've searched. God knows I've looked all over my part of this house. Maybe she's hiding, but I doubt it. She doesn't like to play games. I used to try to get her to play games, but she used to say I was too smart for her, but I know better. She's smarter than me, but she'd been raised not to let men know it because they used to teach girls to do that.

- - -

What say?

- - -

No, I did not look in the basement. She told me to stop going in the goddamn basement. If I do what she tells me not to do, she gets upset. I don't like how I feel when she gets upset. From the front door to our bedroom is thirty steps. From our bedroom to the bathroom is five steps, but that's from my side of the bed and her side of the bed is empty and I miss her being there and pulling the cover off me when she turns over and letting me get cold when the window is open almost every night except when the weather gets cold outside. But seriously, where else would it get cold? Of course, if you want to get technical, it does get cold inside if it's cold enough outside and the heat isn't working then it gets cold inside and she pulls the covers on her side of the bed and she doesn't want to snuggle up close to keep me warm and she isn't here, so it doesn't matter whatsoever. That is another word I used to like—whatsoever. Isn't that a great term? Used to.

- - -

Why do I know all those distances? I keep track of how far it is between places because someday I may go blind. But I know I won't remember so it is a useless exercise. I do it anyway to keep my mind sharp. She used to tell me that it's important when you get old to be able to take care of yourself and not lose things or lose track of where you are or what you're doing.

- - -

No, I don't see any green stuff on that meat.

- - -

Yes, it is okay if your partner looks around. She won't mind even if he goes into her part of the house because she is not here to see him going where she told me not to go. Maybe he will find her.

- - -

Eh?

- - -

No, I never go where she told me not to go.

- - -

No, I don't know how old the dinner is. What does old mean anyway? I don't know, do you? I would like to be certain. I mean, I would like to know, but I don't. I liked being a professor and standing up in front of students and professing even when I didn't know stuff, but I acted like I did, and I guess that's the same as pretending but I got paid. Of course, actors get paid to pretend unless they are amateurs. Isn't it cool to insert a phrase like of course? That tells people I think they're as smart as I am. I hope you're smarter. I don't like talking with somebody who isn't smarter than me because I won't learn anything and that wastes my time. I don't like it when things change, but she is not here and that has changed because she used to be here all the time even when she bothered me.

- - -

What say?

- - -

Yes. She used to bother me.

- - -

I don't how much a lot is.

- - -

No, I have not been eating off that platter. I've been waiting for her, so I can hold her chair. Isn't that a great term? Used to.

- - -

Yes, I think it's beef, but I'm not sure, because I don't know where she is and until I find her it doesn't matter one whit, but I don't know for sure. I don't get to use that word often, but I like it. I used to have a friend named Whit, but I think he is dead because that was long ago when we were college students. Whit was a poet, and he had three children. He would tell people he had one of each and they used to laugh. He was a funny person and I used to like him. I think she would have liked him too, but she's not here, and I don't know where she is because I can't find her.

- - -

What do I eat? Cereal. I like cereal, but I'm tired of it. I'm waiting for her to come back and cook like she used to.

- - -

No, I don't think I can tell you what I've been doing since I couldn't find her because I'm not sure I remember. I have questions about whether God exists in my world. I know God exists in some world because I hear people saying my God, and that's okay, but I'm not sure. I can't burden you with what I've been doing all alone, by myself. When she was here, I was an old man and I'm older now than before she wasn't here anymore. I don't know where she is so I think she must have left when I went to take my walk, she was here in the kitchen cooking my dinner just like she always has done since we got married a long time ago. Of course, she was younger then and didn't get lost from me between when she started to make my supper and when I came back from taking my walk. She was the one who wanted a dog and not me because I used to have lots of dogs when I was a kid and she didn't even though her father wanted her to but her mother didn't and she said she had to check the furnace filter because I could not go down the goddamn steps to the goddamn basement she didn't want me to go down there because I might fall and she would be all alone and now I'm the one who is all alone because she isn't here like she used to be.

- - -

Yes, I opened that wine. She told me not to drink it unless we were together, so I won't. Have I told you the counter in the bathroom is twelve feet four inches from one end to the other? There is one sink for her and one for me and hers is dry and I can't remember when it was wet the last time because she isn't here to tell me. The people who made the counter told her twelve feet four inches was not a standard length, but she said that was okay because she was not a standard person, and that is the truth. She is not a standard person because a standard person would be here with her husband eating the dinner she prepared for him. But she's not, and I don't know where she is although I've looked all over for her, and she is not where she's supposed to be in this house with me.

- - -

What say?

- - -

Yes, I miss her because she listens to me when I talk which is a lot of the time even when I think I should be quiet. It's harder for me to be quiet than it used to be. Most of the time, I liked that because it felt good, but it does not feel good sitting here with her not in the room with me and I don't know where she is or when she'll eat the dinner she cooked for me—us—like she used to do before she went where I can't see her anymore even though you're a nice person it isn't like it used to be when she would listen to me talk. I know you're listening to me talk because you're writing in a notebook like I used to do a long time ago when I was in college with Whit, and he used to make wine and make me laugh only your notebook is black.

- - -

Yes, I liked Whit and I liked his wife. He told me someday I'd find a girl to be my wife and to leave his alone and I did, but now I can't find her and I don't know where she is and I hope you came to help me look for her because I miss her and it isn't fun for me for her to be where I can't find her.

- - -

What? Could you repeat that?

- - -

No, I don't mind if you join your partner for a few minutes. I'll sit here and wait for you. I'm used to waiting.

- - -

What?

- - -

No. I think I'd better not go to the station with you. I promised I would always be here for her, no matter what.

- - -

What?

- - -

No, it's alright. I'll go with you. She used to tell me someday the authorities would take me away, and she was always right when she used to tell me what to do, even though sometimes it was not what I wanted to do.

CHIPMUNKS AND BLUEBIRDS

People have told me that I tend to scowl. Despite appearances, I am a happy person, admittedly happier some days than others. There is something about spring that encourages happiness, and I always look forward to it. This year, spring is more welcome than usual because it promises relief from the anguish of these past several years.

The truth is anguish is an exaggeration. I am not suffering from pain or disease. So, torment is more accurate. For some time now, I have had a nagging feeling that despite following the guidance of a landscaper, we chose the wrong shrubbery for our yard. It may be that the kind of shrubbery makes no difference, but for some reason, we created a wildlife haven in our yard and a persistently worrisome problem. Chipmunks.

Yes, that first cute little chipmunk was welcome, and like most folks, I found it delightful and often amusing. Then there were two. Together they were comical and genuinely fun to watch. Then there were three, then four. The more there were, the more they scurried about the yard—never still long enough for me to count them.

Whoever decided to call a group of chipmunks a scurry knew what she was doing. One chipmunk can scurry around, and two may scurry more. A landscaped yard can withstand only so many of the cute little devils scurrying and digging all those holes to make tunnels, build nests, gnaw at plant roots, and undermine house foundations. And they can get annoyingly noisy—even for a man with hearing loss.

Admittedly, a dozen scurrying chipmunks might provide a few moments of amusement for some folks, not, however, if you are the property owner or gardener who has invested time or money in your landscape. I was both, and they didn't.

Because of job-related moves, we did not live in one place long enough to become familiar with local wildlife eccentricities and cycles. A few years before retirement, we moved to the Atlanta suburbs into a home adjacent to an undeveloped tract with its own Hundred Acre Wood. I planted a small vegetable garden and deployed my first-ever birdfeeders.

For five years, the garden attracted insects and deer, and I learned that deer eat tomatoes. The feeders were less work and more productive. They drew a multitude of colorful and happy-sounding birds and a few squirrels. My hearing was fading, and I missed a lot of the bird songs, but I learned to identify birds by sight and reinforced that humankind can do little to deter squirrels. If the place had chipmunks, they stayed out of my sight. At last, retirement crept into place, and we chose to live in the North Georgia mountains for the usual reasons—a beautiful setting, pleasant climate, and so on. Abundant wildlife came as a bonus, except for the chipmunks.

The creatures like to burrow around the deer-resistant plants near our house. Deer resistance means nothing to chipmunks. Don't ask me why, but it could be that if a shrub is deer resistant, it may be an attraction for chipmunks. I enjoyed watching the little clowns frolic around the yard. Then I noticed a tunnel entrance those devious little devils had cleverly hidden with the fallen leaves. My curiosity drove me to look more closely at what my leaf blower uncovered. There were chipmunk holes in too many places, including on both sides of the garage.

Forget their ability to amuse. They were no longer cute. They had become a nuisance, and while I wondered in vain what caused this plague upon our yard, I decided to remove them and set a trap. That, too, was to no avail. They ignored the bait, but I did trap a bird, which happily flew away when I released it.

After experimenting with several different baits, I tried sunflower seeds, and soon a dozen of the critters found themselves living miles away. Problem solved.

Chipmunks were rare around the yard for a few years, though the neighbor's cat may have been more responsible for my good fortune than the traps. But the burrowers came back, and now the yard is alive with the little beasts and their monotonous chip-chip noise that even I, a man with impaired hearing, can't help but hear.

There is not much hope that the hawks or a cat will rescue me. I haven't seen a hawk in months, and the neighbor moved away and took his cat. Coyotes don't come around anymore. If the snakes are working on my problem, the chipmunks are winning. We have loved and enjoyed cats in the past, but Tommy, our dog, doesn't like the idea of a cat. And he ignores the chipmunks.

A few days ago, I was walking Tommy and considering possible remedies, and the more I pondered, the unhappier I became. A neighbor stopped to chat, and I grumbled about the chipmunk situation. He lamented his own problems, which were much worse than mine. He offered no help and did not lift my mood. Happy hour arrived, and it made sense to go home and partake.

While little Tommy went to the side of the road to do what dogs do at the side of the road, I stood admiring our yard. In addition to azalea and dogwood blooms and colorful spring foliage, several bird species flittered, and four or five squirrels romped and chased each other. They put on a delightful show that lightened my mood, even though I knew it meant more squirrels to come. I recalled squirrels and chipmunks were rare in our neighborhood only a couple of years ago. That fall, we had a bumper crop of nuts. Maybe acorns will be scarcer this year, and we will have fewer chipmunks next spring—or none.

While I watched nature's show, one of the hateful, chipping rodents scurried across the road into our yard. Another followed, and at least three more appeared scattered among the shrubs. My mood darkened, and I longed to see hawks or cats.

A bird landed on a nearby branch. It was the first bluebird I had sighted in our yard this year. Immediately, I felt better and stood appreciating the moment. A lack of human-made noise is one of the joys of our neighborhood. The bird opened its mouth, and its song made my spirits soar. My hearing has almost gone, and bird sounds are audible only under the quietest conditions. Elated is not exaggerating what I felt as I walked into the house.

The scurry of chipmunks may be on the verge of wreaking havoc, but I had heard the bluebird of happiness and decided to worry about the chipmunks some other day—maybe after I install a couple of bluebird houses around the yard.

TROUBLE

Old age keeps me from getting out among people as much as I'd like. Days go by, and other than a daily walk, I stay inside, somewhat isolated. It is not surprising that I move slower, and time moves faster than it used to, but getting slow on the uptake is a surprise and a disappointment.

Like earlier today, I walked into a coffee shop. The barista took my order and said, "You keeping out of trouble?"

Years ago, I heard that question often, a commonplace offered to acknowledge a friend not seen lately. No one expected an honest answer. The question was the same as "How's it going?" A simple acknowledgment, "fine" or "great," did the job. No one wanted to hear a thoughtful answer, certainly not a detailed one. Your entire world may be falling apart, but folks just don't want to hear it from you. That doesn't mean they don't want to know. They may be curious, but it's less personal and less boring to hear the details of your troubles from someone else.

The shop was dimly lit, but her light-blue eyes sparkled in the sunlight through the window. Her question caught me off guard, and her smile seemed genuine. For a fleeting moment, I thought she might find me attractive.

I said, "Nobody has asked me that in years, probably decades."

Her response made me half believe my thought could be true, "Maybe so, but, to me, you look like a fella who could get into a lot of trouble."

"Some people have a gift for seeing people the way they really are, but I have to say I think you're not one of them."

"Oh! Why is that?"

"I haven't been in trouble for years. Decades."

"But you have been in trouble."

"Well, yes."

"Because of something you did, right?"

"Yeah."

"So, there you go. If it happened once, chances are it'll happen again. So, you be careful now." She snapped the top onto my coffee, pushed it across the counter, and said, "Come back to see us."

The exchange lasted two or three minutes. As I walked to the car with my coffee I thought, what a pleasant chat. She seemed like a bright woman, and she made my time in the shop memorable. The problem is her question, and my answer reminded me I did get into trouble a long time ago, and I still don't want to talk or even think about it. So, next time someone asks if I'm keeping out of trouble, I'll just say, "Yes."

ILLUSTRATIONS

Made in the USA
Columbia, SC
30 November 2021

50000892R00081